FROM

ELEMENTAL

AUTUMN
PUBLISHING

Published in 2023
First published in the UK by Autumn Publishing
An imprint of Igloo Books Ltd
Cottage Farm, NN6 0BJ, UK
Owned by Bonnier Books
Sveavägen 56, Stockholm, Sweden
www.igloobooks.com

0623 001
2 4 6 8 10 9 7 5 3 1
ISBN 978-1-83795-848-1

Printed and manufactured in the UK

FROM THE MOVIE

Disney · PIXAR

ELEMENTAL

THE JUNIOR NOVEL

Adapted by Erin Falligant

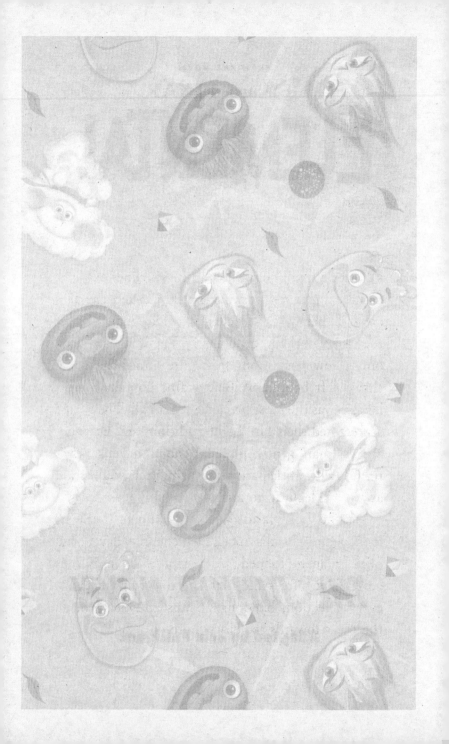

Prologue

Aboard a small boat, the flaming outlines of a Fire couple, a man and a woman, illuminated the area around them. They excitedly awaited the view of the shores of their new country. They travelled with only a few possessions from Fire Land, the home they'd left behind. A Blue Flame contained by a lantern was the most precious item of all. The Flame represented their Fire Land traditions and heritage.

The man gently placed a hand on his wife's round belly, anticipating the baby that would soon arrive. He leant in to talk to it.

As the boat headed towards shore, the man looked into the distance. Element City lay ahead – skyscrapers topped with windmills, buildings covered with trees and high-speed waterways. From every direction, balloons, blimps and boats made their way towards the city's shore.

For the citizens of Element City, it was a typical day. There were all kinds of people here – they were called Elements. Water Elements in varying shades of blue sloshed along pavements. Earth Elements covered in grass, leaves and branches also filled the pavements. Air Elements shaped like colourful clouds drifted past or blew by overhead.

As the boat neared land, the man gently turned his wife to face the shoreline, showing the baby-to-be where they were headed.

He smiled just as the boat reached land. The couple stepped off the boat, relieved to be back on dry, solid ground.

Another boat docked nearby, filled with so many leafy Earth Elements that the ship's deck looked like a forest had sprouted on it. The passengers filed out through its gates.

A submarine emerged, too, and water flowed out into a puddle. Suddenly, Water Elements began to take shape from the puddle, gathering their luggage.

"I believe this is yours," said one Water passenger, holding out a briefcase.

"Thanks!" said another, taking the case. "Have a wetter day!"

Overhead, a blimp landed on a perch. A gust of air shot out of a portal, and Air Elements formed from the cloud. As they disembarked, the blimp deflated. Then more passengers boarded, and it puffed back up.

The Fire couple followed the crowd of Earth, Water and Air Elements into the immigration hall. They paused to admire a mural that depicted three Elements – Earth, Air and Water – coming together to form Element City.

Fire was not amongst them.

The Fire couple waited in the long line of immigrants making their way through the hall. The other Elements stepped away from the Fire couple's flaming forms. Water Elements feared being boiled, while Earth Elements worried their leaves and branches would go up in flames if they got too close.

At last, the Fire couple reached the front of the line.

"Next," called the immigration official.

The Fire couple hurried forwards.

"Name?" asked the official.

The man responded in Firish, the language of Fire Land, his words sizzling with excitement. *"Útrí dàr ì Bùrdì,"* he said.

"Fâsh ì Síddèr," the woman said.

The official didn't understand Firish. He thought

for a moment and got an idea. "You know what? Let's just go with Bernie and… Cinder," said the immigration official, pressing his branch nose onto an ink pad and stamping a document. "Welcome to Element City!"

The Fire couple, now known as Bernie and Cinder Lumen, hurried out the doors into the bustling city. As they walked, they gazed at the canals, waterfalls and giant plants that formed the city's infrastructure. It looked so different from Fire Land. They were a *long* way from home.

"Hot logs!" called a vendor. "Hot logs for sale!"

Bernie turned to see Water Elements gliding about on water slides. Other Elements rode paddleboats along the canals that ran between the city blocks lined with skyscrapers. Bernie walked right over a tiny Earth Element. Bernie lifted his leg, but her leaf hair caught on fire. A tiny Earth man walking behind her tried to extinguish it without success. A water person passing by doused them with water from his hand. The Earth woman's hair fire went out and the Earth man sprouted new growth.

They continued walking down the busy street. Distracted by the sights, Bernie walked right through an Air Element.

"Hey! Watch it, Sparky!" cried the Air Element. His legs were separated from his body. They kicked over Bernie and Cinder's suitcase and walked off, rejoining the upper body.

Before Bernie could apologise, a Wetro train zoomed overhead on an elevated track. As the train crossed a bridge, Bernie got an idea.

A few minutes later, he stood beside Cinder inside a crowded train car. The other passengers shrank back and stared.

The narrow train car was not designed for Fire Elements.

When the train lurched, a Water guy stumbled, splashing water onto Cinder. Bernie gasped. Water would damage her flames! As her doused flames sizzled, Bernie quickly fed her some wood from their luggage. Then he glared at the Water guy.

"What?" the guy said with a shrug.

"Hmm," Bernie grumbled. "Water." This was going to be a long ride.

Bernie and Cinder exited the Wetro station in an Earth neighbourhood. When they saw a For Rent sign in the window of an upscale brownstone building, they hurried towards the door. The owner, an old-growth Earth Element, opened the door and his eyes widened.

Cinder gave him a hopeful smile and waved hello. But when her flames set the owner's dry, leafy hair on fire, he quickly closed the door.

At another building, Cinder pushed a buzzer, which instantly caught fire. She blew it out before the owner, a Water Element, opened the door. But when the owner saw the Fire couple – and the smouldering doorbell – they slammed the door shut.

One after another, homeowners turned them away. With each slam of the door, Bernie and Cinder grew more discouraged. But they kept walking.

When they reached a run-down neighbourhood, they sat down to rest. Dejected and tired, they were about to give up. That was when Bernie spotted a shabby building with a For Sale sign in front. Hope flickered in his chest.

Inside the old structure, Bernie's mind raced, full of ideas for their new home. He would turn the first floor into a shop, a shrine to Fire Land where they would sell snacks and souvenirs inspired by their homeland.

Plink! Water dripped from a pipe above, barely missing Cinder's flames.

Bernie didn't notice. He paced so excitedly that his feet burned through the floor, and he fell into the basement. "I'm okay!" he hollered up through the splinters. When Cinder saw his thumbs-up, she smiled with relief.

They placed their Blue Flame lantern in the hearth.

Bernie and Cinder were home.

One evening, it began to rain outside. But inside, their new home felt cosy, warm and full of love.

That night, Cinder gave birth to their baby.

The tiny Fire baby lit up the room.

"Íkì ss ûr," Cinder murmured. "It's a girl."

"Bê ss ksòrìf," said Bernie. "She's so perfect." He reached into the Blue Flame lantern and scooped up some flames to gently pour over the baby's head. She cooed... and then sneezed.

Bernie laughed. He held Ember up so she could see the world around her. "Welcome, my Ember, to your new life," he said.

In the years that followed, Bernie and Cinder adjusted to living in Element City. While they learnt a new language and new ways of doing things, Bernie also taught Ember the language, values and customs of their homeland.

When Bernie carefully poured the Blue Flame into a cauldron, Ember's eyes blazed with interest. "Our Blue Flame holds all our traditions and gives us the strength to burn bright," he explained.

Ember watched as the Flame shot up inside the cauldron.

"Do I burn as bright?" Bernie asked, flexing his muscles and striking one silly pose after another.

Ember giggled. While her father pushed the cauldron against the wall, she rode on it and cheered him on.

Slowly but surely, as Ember grew, the shop began to take shape. Bernie added shelving and repaired the walls. He was eager for the time when his store would be ready.

Soon Ember started helping Bernie with his daily tasks. One day, they made a sign for the front door. Bernie wrote FIREPLACE in large letters on the sign. Then Ember burned a flame design into it with her finger. When it was finished, Bernie climbed a ladder and hung the sign above the shop's entrance.

He climbed down the ladder and stood beside Ember, admiring their work. "This shop is the *dream* of our family," he said. "And someday it will all be yours."

Ember's eyes widened. From that moment on, *this* was what she would strive for, to be a good daughter and to take over the shop – her father's dream.

Chapter 1

A year later, it was opening day at Bernie's shop. The lava java pot was full, and hot logs rolled on a warmer. Bernie stood behind the counter with Ember beside him.

Cinder stocked shelves nearby. When a Fire Element entered, Bernie greeted them. "Welcome! Everything here is authentic."

"Then I gotta try the kol nuts," said the customer.

"Kol nuts coming up!" said Bernie.

While her father rang up the order, Ember tapped the keys on her toy till.

"Good daughter," Bernie said warmly.

He and Ember squeezed logs in their palms to make bite-sized pieces of kol nuts and placed them on a plate. Ember handed the plate to the customer.

"Someday this shop will all be mine!" she announced with pride.

Bernie tousled his daughter's flames. "When you are ready," he said.

As time passed, more people emigrated from Fire Land to the Firetown district of Element City. Bernie's shop grew busier. Most of the customers were Fire Elements, but sometimes other Elements shopped there, too. The busier the shop became, the more Ember helped out. She even assisted Bernie with his deliveries. Ember rode on his shoulders as they buzzed around town on a scooter.

"Delivery!" Bernie announced.

"Delivery!" Ember echoed.

Soon she was old enough to make lollipops, one of her favourite tasks.

On one busy afternoon, two Fire kids approached the counter. One of them ordered two lollipops, placing a few coins on the counter.

"I got it, *Àshfá!*" Ember told her father. She melted a lollipop with the heat from her hands. Then she blew into it, sculpting the pop into a glass-like bubble. While she worked, her inner fire glowed happily. A rainbow-coloured halo shimmered around her.

Ember formed flames at the top of the pop and used her finger to draw on a face. When she was done, the pop looked just like her customer! She tweaked the nose and handed it to the Fire kid, who laughed with delight.

The Fire kid's friend leant over and tried to lick the pop.

"Hey!" snapped the first kid.

Bernie smiled, until two Water teenagers entered the shop. The teens tracked water inside and carelessly bumped into shelves.

Bernie nodded at Ember. "Water," he muttered. "Keep an eye on them."

Ember zipped up her fire as if putting on protective armour. Then she saluted her father. She approached the teens, who were pouring water onto some flaming souvenirs.

"Oops!" said one teen, giggling as if it were an accident.

"Oops!" said the other as the Blue Flame souvenir in his hand sputtered and smoked.

Ember blazed up beside them. "You splash it, you buy it!" she growled.

One of the Water teens began to boil from her heat. "Ahhh!" he cried. The souvenir popped out of his hand, and Ember caught it just in time.

The teens sloshed out of the shop. Ember watched them go with a satisfied smile.

"You showed them, huh?" said Bernie. He hollered out the door after the teens. "Nobody waters down fire!"

"Yeah!" called Ember.

A few years later, Cinder restocked shelves while a Fire soap opera played on the TV above the counter. "The truth is …," a soap opera actress said dramatically on the screen. The customers in the shop hung on her every word.

Cinder finished folding a KISS ME, I'M FIRISH T-shirt. She glanced at the TV. "She's not in love with him," she guessed.

"… I'm not in love with you!" said the soap opera actress.

The customers in the shop gasped.

"Ha! Knew it!" Cinder boasted.

Behind the counter, Ember helped her father make kol nuts. Now that she was a teenager, she was even faster than him! While he struggled to compress the logs into kol nuts, she effortlessly stacked up a pile of the tasty burnt nuts.

When a man with thick glasses approached, Ember nudged her father. *"Àshfá,"* she said. "Customer."

Bernie hesitated. "How about," he said, "you take it today."

"For real?" she asked, beaming. She had been waiting to hear those words for a long time. She wiped her hands on her apron and took a deep breath as she welcomed the customer.

"How can I help you?" she asked with a smile.

The customer placed a metal basket filled with items on the counter, next to a bucket of sparklers. "All this," he said. "And sparklers are 'buy one, get one free'?"

"That's right!" said Ember.

"Great! I'll take the free one," said the customer. He grabbed a sparkler out of the bucket and lit it with his finger.

Ember laughed nervously. "Oh, no, see… you need to *buy* one to get one free." She gently took the sparkler from the customer's grip. Then she blew it out.

"But I just want the free one," he insisted, taking another sparkler.

"Sorry," said Ember, plastering on a smile. "That's not how this works." She grabbed the sparkler from his hand and blew it out.

"But the customer is always right," he snapped.

"Not in this case…," said Ember.

He took another sparkler. Ember took it away. He grabbed another, and she took it away. "Nope," she said, blowing out the sparklers. Soon she had a bouquet of burnt-out sparklers in her hand. "Nope, nope, nope, nope, nope!"

"Just give me one for free!" demanded the customer.

"That's not how this works!" Ember bellowed. Her flames flickered, turning purple, and then…

KABOOM!

She exploded.

By the time the blast cleared, the shopping basket on the counter had melted into a smoky blob. A black scorch mark was streaked across the floor, and little fires burned throughout the shop.

"Oh!" said Bernie, hurrying over. He grabbed some sparklers from the bucket and stuck them into the melty blob. Then he blew on them to light them and handed the blob to the customer. "Happy birthday!"

Bernie walked a shocked Ember away from the counter. "What just happened?" he asked. "Why did you lose your temper?"

"I… I don't know," Ember sputtered. "He was pushing and pushing, and it just…"

15

"Calm, calm," said Bernie. "Sometimes customers can be tough. Just take a breath and make a connection."

Ember nodded.

"When you can do that and not lose your temper, then you will be ready to take over the shop," said Bernie.

Ember forced a smile. She could do this. She *would* do this.

Chapter 2

Many years later, Ember still recalled her father's words when she had a difficult customer – like right now.

Take a breath, make a connection, she told herself. But her face flamed bright red with licks of purple. Take a breath, *make a connection...* She tried again. *Take a breath! MAKE A CONNECTION!*

Too late.

KABLAM! She exploded, smashing the shop's glass worktop.

Ember waved the smoke away and cast an apologetic look at the shocked customer.

"Sorry," Ember said with an embarrassed laugh. "Sorry about that. Sorry, sorry."

Two Fire shop regulars, Flarry and Flarrietta sat nearby. "She almost went full purple!" said Flarrietta. "I've never seen anyone go full purple!"

"Sorry, everyone," called Ember as her father hurried over.

"Oh! Please forgive my daughter," Bernie added. "She burns bright, but sometimes *too* bright."

He blew out a burning flower on the customer's hat. "Nice hat, by the way," he said. "Let me make you a new batch! On the house!"

The customer nodded. But she turned on her heel and walked away.

Bernie started making the kol nuts while Ember scooped up the broken glass.

"Sorry, *Àshfá*," she said. "I don't know why that one got away from me." She put the glass in her mouth and started chewing.

"Oh, you are tense because of the big Red Dot Sale tomorrow," said her father. "It has us all worked up."

"I guess," she admitted. Ember finished chewing and blew the glass into a long glowing tube. She flattened the glass into a pane. "It's just... some of these customers get me all... *grrr*."

"I know, I know. Just do what we practised," said her father. "You are *so* good at everything else."

"You're right," said Ember. "I'll get it. I just want you to rest." With one last inhale, she put the final touches on the glass pane.

"Mm-hmm," she said, feeling proud of her work. She slid the glass back into the worktop with a satisfied sigh. "Done."

Bernie continued to make kol nuts, but then he started coughing.

"You okay?" asked Ember.

Bernie sniffed. "Just tired."

"Let me help," insisted Ember.

Bernie caught his breath while Ember finished making the nuts.

From across the shop Flarry called, "Bernie, that cough is terrible."

"Almost as terrible as your cooking," said Flarrietta.

Bernie laughed. "*Ê... shútsh,*" he said. "Sheesh."

"When you gonna put Ember out of her misery and retire, huh?" asked Flarrietta. "Finally put her name on the sign out there?"

Ember listened. When *would* her father retire?

"She will take over when she's ready," Bernie simply replied.

Ember cracked a joke to hide her disappointment. "And speaking of 'ready', we are *more* than ready for you to actually *buy* something," she told Flarrietta, "if you'd ever get up off your lazy ash."

Everyone in the shop burst into laughter. "Oh!" they called. "Burn!"

Bernie smiled. "But she is *so* close," he admitted. "I mean, she'll probably never do deliveries as quick as me..."

Everyone laughed again.

"... but actions speak louder than worms," he continued.

"Words," corrected Ember.

"Words!" Bernie echoed.

"You don't think I can beat your record?" She picked up a timer, cranking the dial. "Because I've been taking it easy on you so I don't hurt your feelings, Mr Smokestack. But game on!"

As the timer ticked, Ember hurried to pack up the deliveries. Bernie watched, a proud smile flickering across his face.

Chapter 3

Cinder sat in her cosy office. As Firetown's self-appointed matchmaker, she had a natural gift for smelling love. She could tell, without a doubt, when two people might make a good match... or not.

Cinder gazed across the table at a young, nervous Fire couple. "Before I see if you are a match," she began, "I will splash this on your heart to bring love to the surface."

She stirred a bowl of oil and splashed a few drops onto the couple. Their flames blazed red. Then the couple lit the two sticks that Cinder had set on the table.

"And I will read the smoke," continued Cinder. She sniffed the wisps of smoke rising from the sticks.

Just then, Ember threw open the curtains in the room. *Whoosh!* The smoke dissipated.

"Ember!" scolded Cinder. "I'm doing a reading!"

"Sorry," said Ember. "Gotta grab some stuff.

Going for Dad's record." She raced towards the boxes in a corner of the room.

"So… are we a match?" asked the Fire guy.

"It's true love!" Cinder announced. "Which is more than I ever smelt on this one." She shot Ember a look.

Ember rolled her eyes. "Oh, goodie. This ol' chestnut."

As Ember turned to leave, Cinder grabbed her daughter's arm and sniffed it. "Yup, nothing," Cinder confirmed. "Just a loveless, sad future of sadness."

Ember pulled her arm free and started walking out of the room.

"Ember!" her mother called. "Work with me!"

Ember rolled her eyes again and sighed.

"You finding a match was my mother's dying wish!" Cinder said, her voice crackling. She reminded Ember of the day Ember's grandmother had died. "Promise me one thing. Marry Fire," her grandmother had said. And then… *poof!* She was gone.

"Nice try, Mum," said Ember. "Gotta go!"

When Cinder turned back towards the Fire couple, they were embracing. She squirted them with a spray bottle. "Save it for the wedding!" she spat.

"Hey!" the Fire guy sputtered.

Outside the shop, Ember carried the boxes to her scooter. That was when Clod, a young Earth boy, popped out of a planter. His camo-coloured shirt matched the green grass sprouting from his head.

"Yo, yo, yo, Ember!" he called.

"Yo, Clod. Can't talk. In a hurry," she said. "And don't let my dad catch you out here again."

"What?" he said, giving his hair a quick comb with a gardening fork. "He doesn't like my *land*scaping?"

"Uff," groaned Ember at the joke. She strapped the boxes to her scooter.

"Anyway," said Clod, "June Bloom is coming, and you just got to be my date. 'Cause check it out – I'm all grown up!" He lifted his arm, revealing a tiny flower that had sprouted in his armpit. He sniffed it. "And I smell *gooood*."

As Clod plucked the flower, he let out an "Ow!" Then he knelt on the pavement and offered it to Ember in a grand gesture.

"My queen."

Ember took the flower. *Poof!* It burnt to a crisp in her hand. "Sorry, buddy," she said. "Elements don't mix."

Then she remembered – the timer was ticking! "Flame! Gotta go!"

"Come on!" Clod begged. "Go to the festival with me! You *never* leave this part of town."

"That's because everything I need is right here," replied Ember.

Just then, a Wetro train passed overhead, sending water splashing down. Ember glanced up, annoyed, as she popped open her umbrella.

"Plus," she said, "this city wasn't made with Fire people in mind."

As the train crossed the bridge towards Element City, Ember closed the umbrella and climbed onto her scooter.

"Sorry," she told Clod, "but it'd take an act of God to get me to cross that bridge."

"An act of God, or an act of... *Clod*?" He waggled his eyebrows.

Ember didn't bother to laugh. "Gotta run!" she said as she drove away.

She arrived at the grocery store first, handing a delivery to a Fire Element, who rushed out to give her a gift. Next, she delivered a package to the Fire chef at a food stall. Then she stopped alongside a Fire couple pushing a charcoal grill.

Ember handed them a bottle filled with lighter fluid. "As ordered," she said with a smile.

The couple lifted the lid off the grill, revealing a

tiny Fire baby being warmed by the coals. The baby grabbed the bottle and sucked it down, burping up flames.

"Gotta run!" said Ember. "Going for Dad's record."

The tension Ember felt at the shop melted away while she made deliveries. But as she pulled into traffic behind an old truck, she quickly lost her patience.

"Move it!" she hollered. She revved her scooter and manoeuvred it around the truck. She shook her fist. *"Sháshà r íshà!"* she hollered. "Spark in the dirt!"

Delivery after delivery, Ember worked as quickly as she could. She placed sandbags in the arms of the owner of a smoke-cleaner shop. She handed off a parcel outside a woodshop. She dropped off a box of fireworks at a fireworks store. Fire kids standing nearby swarmed around the box. The fireworks exploded to the delight of the kids.

But Ember didn't have time to enjoy the show. As the fireworks lit up the sky, she happily raced home.

When she reached the shop, a Closed sign hung on the door. Ember hurried inside and saw that the timer hadn't yet gone off. "Ha, ha!" she called to her father with a smile. "Winner, winner, charcoal dinner!"

But Bernie was asleep at the counter, surrounded by paperwork and red dot stickers.

Ember toned down her celebration and tiptoed across the floor, trying not to wake her father. Her smile faded when she saw how old Bernie looked. *She* was the reason he hadn't been able to retire. Because she wasn't ready. Because she still lost her temper.

When she draped a chain mail shawl over his shoulders, Bernie woke with a smoky cough. Ember gently pulled a red dot sticker off his cheek.

"Head to bed," she said. "I'll close things up." She helped her father stand.

"I still have much to prepare for the Red Dot Sale," he argued.

"Dad, I'll take care of it," she insisted. "You need to rest."

Just then, the timer rang out. Bernie glanced at it with surprise, understanding that Ember had beaten his record! "How?" he asked.

Ember shrugged. "I learnt from the best."

They both laughed. Then Ember led her father across the shop. As they passed the Blue Flame, Bernie coughed again.

"I am old," he said with a sigh. "I can't do this forever." He picked up a twig from the stack at the base of the Blue Flame's cauldron. "Now that you have beaten my time, there is only one thing you haven't done. Tomorrow I will sleep in. And I want *you* to run the shop for the Red Dot Sale."

Ember gasped. "Seriously? By myself?"

Bernie broke the twig in two and handed half to Ember. "If you can do that without losing your temper," he challenged her, "it will show me you are able to take over."

Ember stood tall. "You got it, *Àshfá*," she said.

Bernie held the twig with both hands and closed his eyes. Then he tossed it into the Blue Flame.

"I won't let you down," said Ember. "I swear. You'll see."

Bernie patted her shoulder. "Hmm," he said. "Good daughter."

As he trudged up the stairs, Ember watched him go. Then she did a happy dance. "Yes!" she cried out.

When she turned back to the Blue Flame, she held her stick and closed her eyes. Before she tossed the stick into the cauldron, she whispered, "Blue Flame, please let this go my way."

Chapter 4

Early the next morning, the streets of Firetown were calm. But inside Bernie's shop, Ember was hard at work, slapping stickers onto various items.

When it was time to open, she adjusted the Red Dot Sale pin on her apron. "Take a breath," she reminded herself. "Calm as a candle."

When she rolled up the shade on the window, a crowd of customers was waiting, but Ember kept her cool. She smiled and opened the door.

"Morning," she said. "Welcome to the Fireplace—"

Before she could finish, customers rushed in, practically trampling her flames.

One customer headed towards some cans arranged in a pyramid. Instead of taking the top can, the customer yanked one out from the bottom. As the stack wobbled, Ember hurried over.

"Whoa, whoa!" she cried. "They're all the same.

Just take one from the top." She handed a can to the customer. "Thanks for shopping!"

Another customer heaved an armload of red stickers onto the counter. "So many stickers for sale!" the customer grunted.

"Are these fragile?" asked another customer as they swept a shelf of delicate items into their basket.

"No, wait!" cried Ember – too late.

Smash! Several shattered on the floor.

Ember stifled a yell. She tried to calm herself and keep her cool. Then she saw another customer about to put a log in their mouth – without even paying! "You have to pay before you eat," she reminded them, yanking the log away.

The morning passed by in a blur. Amid the endless stream of customers and the constant *ring* of the till, Ember tried to stay calm. Her father was counting on her. But the customers had so many questions!

"Does this come in a large?"

"What's your return policy?"

"Has anyone seen my husband?"

Ember's flames turned bright red. *Take a breath,* she reminded herself.

"My dad broke this," said a Fire child, holding up a damaged toy.

Make connection, Ember told herself through gritted teeth.

"Mind if I test this kettle?" asked a customer, just as the kettle released a high-pitched whistle.

Ember was about to blow her top, too. It was all too much.

She strained to keep her cool. But any moment now, she'd blow. She could almost *feel* her flames turning purple.

"Back in five minutes!" Ember choked out through gritted teeth.

She rushed from the room, her hand clamped over her mouth and sparks flying. She made it down the basement steps. Then she let out a fiery blast. "Ahhhhhh!"

As the smoke cleared, Ember panted, trying to recover. That was when a pipe in the basement began to vibrate.

The pipe groaned, squealed, and then... cracked. *Whoosh!* It shot a stream of water straight at Ember.

Ouch! She ducked as it doused part of her flame.

More water gushed from the pipe, quickly flooding the floor. Ember gasped when the brick support column in the middle of the basement shuddered.

As water continued to fill the basement, Ember

dodged the painful spray. She had to do something before the situation got even worse. Thinking fast, she grabbed a rubbish bin lid and a fireplace poker. She climbed onto some floating debris and then reached towards the cracked pipe.

Water stung her flames as she pushed the lid against the broken pipe, stopping the spray. She melted the poker in her hand and used it to weld the edges of the lid against the pipe. Then she held her breath and released her grip.

The lid stayed put. The water stopped!

But as Ember glanced around the water-logged basement, she began to panic. "Oh, no. Stupid temper. Not today!"

Her own flame was damaged, too. She grabbed a few sticks from a shelf and ate them, replenishing her flame. "What is wrong with me?" she cried.

A picture frame floated on the water. When it began to move, Ember sucked in her breath. Two streams of water fountained up out of the pool and two watery hands appeared, holding the frame. Then Wade Ripple, a young Water man, sat up. He was bawling his eyes out!

Ember gasped. "What the...?" she said.

Wade studied the picture in the frame and cried some more. "What a happy family," he said, sniffling. "Is that you and your *dad*?" He pointed at the picture of Ember sitting on her father's lap, blowing out birthday candles. "I love dads. And it's your birthday!" He cried so hard now, his tears splashed Ember.

She winced, shielding her face. "Who are you?" she demanded. "What are you doing here?"

"I don't know!" Wade sobbed. "I was searching for a leak on the other side of the river and got sucked in. This is bad! I can't lose another job! I just can't seem to find my flow."

When he stood, Ember couldn't help noticing that he was tall and *very* muscular. "Dang," she whispered. Her flames burned pink.

Wade glanced down. "Ugh, that pipe squished me all out of shape," he said. He shook his body until the muscles disappeared and his belly plopped back out. "That's better."

"Dude, just get out of here," Ember pleaded, growing impatient now. "I gotta clean this mess before my dad sees what I did."

Wade stopped crying and straightened up. "Oh, actually...," he said, sloshing towards the other side of the room. He grabbed a pen and notepad from under his shirt. "I'm afraid I'm going to have to write you a ticket."

"A ticket?" cried Ember.

"Yeah, I'm a city inspector," said Wade. "And this pipe is definitely not up to code."

Ember held her face with her hands. "I sucked a city inspector into our pipes?"

"I know – ironic, right?" said Wade. He poked at the pipe, which rumbled.

"Stop messing with that!" cried Ember.

"I need to make sure it's solid," Wade explained.

"It's solid," Ember confirmed. "I should know. My dad built it himself."

"Wait," said Wade, glancing up. "Your dad did?"

"Yes! With his bare hands," said Ember with pride. "Every brick and board. This place was a ruin when he found it."

"Wow, he did all of this himself?" asked Wade. "Without permits?" He began to weep again.

Ember gulped. "Uh…"

"I'm gonna have to write that up, too," said Wade. "First I'm sucked into a pipe, and now I have to write citations that could get this place shut down. Oh gosh, it's just too much!" Tears streamed from his eyes.

Ember flared up. "Shut us *down*?"

"I know!" wailed Wade. "It's awful!"

"No! You can't shut us down," Ember begged.

"Please! This is a big day for me. It's our Red Dot Sale!" She lunged for Wade's notepad.

"Hey, take it easy," he said, flowing out of her path. "This is as hard on me as it is on you." He scribbled furiously on his pad. He sloshed towards the basement window.

"Get back here!" cried Ember.

"Sorry," said Wade. "I gotta get these to City Hall before the end of my shift." Without another word, he poured his body through the high, narrow window and disappeared.

Ember was right behind him. She ripped off her apron. Then she blazed through the window and chased after Wade. "Get back here!"

At that moment, a pipe joint began to leak.

But Ember didn't notice.

Chapter 5

From the shop, Bernie glanced through the window – just in time to see Ember chasing a Water man down the street. "Hmm?" Bernie asked aloud.

Ember followed Wade towards the Wetro station and the bridge that she had told Clod would take an act of God for her to cross. But as Wade boarded a train, Ember knew she had to follow.

"Next stop, Element City!" the announcer's voice rang out.

As the doors of the last train car started to close, Ember pulled her hood over her flames and stepped inside.

She scanned the crowd for Wade. Ember tried to squeeze past a huge, grassy Earth Element, but when the train lurched, she accidentally slammed into the Earth man.

Poof! His grass burnt up, leaving a very skinny guy. "Hay!" he cried.

"Sorry!" said Ember.

Then she spotted Wade ahead. The train car was too crowded for her to squeeze through. Thinking fast, she climbed out a window.

As Ember inched along the outside of the car, wind whipped her flames. Then Ember saw water splash from an aqueduct ahead. The train was about to pass under a giant waterfall!

She gasped and melted her way in through a window – just in time. She fell to the floor, trying to catch her breath.

The train car turned pitch black as it barrelled through a tunnel. Ember was the only light source in the train. As she blazed through the car, searching for Wade, other passengers turned in surprise.

Suddenly, Ember saw a flame hovering in front of her. Puzzled, she reached her hand towards the flames. "Huh? What the…?"

That was when the train burst out of the tunnel. As light flooded the train car, Ember saw that the other Fire Element was her own reflection flickering at the back of Wade's head!

Wade held a thick stack of tickets in his hand – tickets that could shut down Bernie's shop. As Ember reached for them, Wade's hand boiled at her heat.

"This stop, City Hall," announced a bored-sounding voice as the train rolled into the Wetro station.

Wade glanced down at his boiling hand. "Ah!" he cried, whirling around. "Hands off!" He whipped the tickets away from Ember and raced out of the train car.

"Gah!" Ember exited too, dodging passengers boarding the train and apologising along the way.

Wade streamed easily down the crowded stairs, but Ember struggled to follow. "Ugh," she muttered. "Stop!" As she tried to hurry, she collided with other passengers.

"Stop!" she cried again, but Wade was too far away. She reached the street at the same time as an Air Element, who floated into the path of a passing car. *Poof!*

When the Air Element reformed, his jacket was on the ground. "Aw! My new jacket," he muttered as he drifted away.

Ember blazed across the street and down the pavement after Wade. He passed a nursery-school bus and then streamed through a crowd of Earth kids.

The kids blocked Ember's path. Thinking fast, Ember popped open her umbrella and fired up her flames. Like a hot-air balloon, she floated high over the kids, gazing down at their amazed faces.

But when her umbrella melted, she tumbled to the ground, landing on some rubbish bins. She pushed herself up and chased after Wade.

Wade saw Ember coming. He took a sharp left.

Ember skidded to a stop and saw that he had slipped into a narrow space between two buildings. She squeezed in her flames and shimmied after him.

They both worked their way through the tight passageway.

Wade reached the opening on the other side, but his ticket book got caught in a crevice. He grunted, trying to pull it out. It finally gave way, and he splashed onto the pavement.

Moments later, Ember emerged, too. As she and Wade raced towards City Hall, she swiped a bottle of chilli oil from a dirt burger vendor's cart.

"Huh?" said the vendor.

Ember blazed ahead until she was in Wade's path. She squirted the chilli oil onto the pavement. The oil fed her flames, creating a huge wall of fire.

"Come on, guy," she said. "You can't get through this. So it is time to hand 'em over."

"Oh, boy," he said. "I'm sorry. This is going to be really disappointing for you."

He sloshed forwards and poured down through a nearby pavement grate. Then he spouted up through another grate past Ember. He gave her one last look as she watched him step into the revolving doors of City Hall.

"No, no, no, no, no, no!" cried Ember.

"Sorry!" called Wade.

Ember's flame dimmed with despair. "Please! No!" she hollered after him. "You don't understand."

As her shoulders slumped, her inner prismatic light glowed like a sad, weary rainbow.

Inside the building, Wade placed his tickets in a canister. He loaded the canister into a vacuum tube and let it go. *Foomp!* Then he noticed flecks of colourful light dancing across the wall.

"Whoa," said Wade. He glanced out the window to find the source of the light.

It was Ember, just outside the door. "The shop is my dad's dream," she was saying, more to herself than to him. "If I'm the reason it gets shut down, it will kill him. He will never trust me to take over."

"Aw," Wade murmured. He held a hand to his chest, his face covered in tears, and stepped outside.

"Why didn't you say that before?" he asked Ember.

She zipped up her fire, shield on. "Wait, does that mean you'll tear up the tickets?" she asked.

"I mean, I would," said Wade. "But I just sent them over to the processing department." He gestured towards the vacuum tube system inside the doors.

Ember growled and held her head in frustration.

Wade spoke quickly. "But I can take you there so you can plead your case!"

Ember perked up, hope flickering in her chest.

Chapter 6

Ember followed Wade into an office filled with tangled, leafy vines. She could barely see through the thick jungle of stalks and leaves. When Wade pushed past a branch, it snapped back at Ember.

"Whoa!" she cried, ducking.

At the back of the office, a large Earth guy sat at a cluttered desk with a nameplate that read FERN GROUCHWOOD. His overgrown leaves sprouted this way and that. Only his grassy moustache appeared tidy and trimmed.

"Hey, Fern!" said Wade with a bright smile. "How you doing?"

"Living the dream," mumbled Fern. On the tree-stump desk before him, his inbox overflowed with papers. Behind him, vacuum tubes lined the wall.

Wade laughed nervously. "You know those citations I just sent you from Firetown?"

Fern held up a metal canister filled with forms. "I was about to send them to Mrs Cumulus," he said slowly, "then get sprayed for fungus rot." He started to put the canister into a tube.

"Wait!" cried Ember.

Fern hesitated.

"Before you do," said Wade, "maybe she could have a word?" He nodded to Ember.

She leant across the desk towards Fern. "Hi...," she began with a smile. But then... *hiss!* Her hot hands singed the wooden desk, leaving handprints. "Whoa!" she cried, stepping backwards.

Fern stared at her, unamused.

Ember tried to sound bright and breezy. "Look, I know that we have some non-permitted stuff in our shop," she said. She winked at the word *non-permitted*. "But who doesn't skate around permits sometimes?" She laughed and raised her hand. "Guilty."

Fern didn't even crack a smile. "You realise you're saying this, out loud, to the actual permit office, right?" He started again to put the canister into the tube.

"Wait!" cried Ember and Wade at the exact same time.

"Tell him what you told me, about your dad and letting him down," said Wade quickly.

"No!" snapped Ember, flaring up. "That's personal!"

Wade leant backwards, away from her hot flames. "It really got to me. He might feel it, too." He started to tell the story himself. "Her dad will be super—" he began.

"Nope!" Ember tried to cover his mouth.

But Wade kept talking. "Super—"

"Nope!" said Ember again. She searched for something to stuff into Wade's face.

"Super disa—" he said.

Ember grabbed the nameplate from Fern's desk and shoved it into Wade's mouth. It floated, suspended, in his watery face, but he kept talking.

"—ppointed in her," he somehow managed to say.

Ember's heat rose. She took a deep breath and blew it out in short bursts, trying to calm herself. Then she pleaded with Wade. "Stop it!"

He wouldn't stop talking to Fern, even with the nameplate in his mouth. "He might even be..."

Ember reached for a snow globe from Fern's desk and shoved it into Wade's face, knocking out the nameplate.

His mouth was full now, but Wade eeked out one more word: "… ashamed."

Ember continued her stress-breathing, but it wasn't working. "What are you doing?" She felt her flames start to turn purple.

"But the main thing is if her father can't retire," said Wade, who was weeping now, "it will be all Ember's… f-f-f—"

Fern hung on Wade's every word now, waiting.

But before Wade could finish his sentence, Ember exploded in a ball of fire. "STOP TALKING!" she roared.

When the smoke cleared, Fern's hair was singed black and his grass moustache was gone. His burnt wire-rimmed glasses sat askew on his nose. Everything on Fern's desk had burnt to a crisp, too – except the citations that would shut down Bernie's shop. Those were inside a metal canister.

Wade doused a flaming bobblehead on the desk as Fern studied his scorched inbox. "Looks like I'm going home early today," Fern said flatly. He put the canister into the tube.

"No, don't—" Ember begged, her flames blazing with desperation.

The tickets shot through the vacuum tube. *Foomp!*

"Expect to get shut down within a week," said Fern as he stood. "Have a good one."

On his way out of the office, which now looked like a scorched jungle, he handed Ember a brochure titled *So Your Business Is Being Shut Down.* Ember sighed, feeling absolutely and utterly defeated.

"Sorry," whispered Wade, his eyes teary.

Ember slowly walked home over the bridge, all the way back to the shop. When she got there, she saw the Closed sign hanging on the door. She gasped. "What? Already?"

She burst into the shop.

"Hello?"

When Ember heard her father coughing in the basement, she rushed down the stairs. She couldn't believe what she was seeing. Pipes had burst and were leaking everywhere! Her parents were desperately trying to clean up the mess.

"Oh, no," Ember said. "Dad! What happened?" she asked.

"We are lucky nobody got hurt," Bernie said in a rush. "It *ruined* the Red Dot Sale!"

Ember winced with guilt.

"Did *he* do this?" Bernie cried.

"Who?" asked Ember.

"That Water guy I saw you chase." Water dripped onto Bernie's face from above. He cringed at the sting.

"Oh, uh, um... yeah, he did," Ember fibbed. "He just broke through a pipe. I don't know why. Luckily, I was able to close it off. I, uh, couldn't catch him, though."

Bernie flared with anger. "Water," he spat. "Always trying to water us down!"

"He was a Water *person*, Dad, not just water," she reminded Bernie.

"Same thing," he grumbled. "And why is there water in the pipes? The city shut it down years ago. There should be *no water*!" He coughed again, so violently that he nearly fell backwards.

"Dad!" Ember caught him just before he hit the water.

"Bernie!" Cinder cried out. She led him towards the stairs and rubbed his back. "We will get through this. Just like before."

"Before?" asked Ember.

Cinder sank to the step beside Bernie. "There is a reason we left Fire Land," she said. "Oh, Ember, it was so beautiful there." She smiled at the memory.

"Here in Firetown, we are the only family with a

Blue Flame. But back home, *every* family had one." Cinder described the Blue Flames in the windows, including the one in the restaurant Bernie and Cinder had started in Fire Land. Cinder had been pregnant with Ember then.

"Your father put everything we had into starting our life together. But then a great storm came," Cinder said, her voice grave.

She described how she and Bernie had looked up and seen a storm brewing above the rooftops. Then the ferocious winds had hit.

Debris crashed down inside the restaurant, knocking over the cauldron with the Blue Flame. Bernie had acted quickly, capturing the Flame in a lantern as the restaurant continued to collapse.

"All was lost for us," said Cinder.

After the storm, the restaurant was a pile of rubble. Most of the neighbours' buildings had been damaged, too. "But it was too painful to stay," said Cinder. "We needed to start over, somewhere new."

And so they boarded a boat they had found on the beach. Bernie's parents watched as the boat pulled away from the shore. "It was the last time your father ever saw his family," said Cinder, her voice heavy. "That is why we came here. To build this. Our new life."

Bernie was mopping the floor now, but he listened with tears in his eyes. Ember had never seen him so emotional. She looked at the brochure from Fern and felt her fire reignite.

"*Àshfá*, nothing will happen to this shop or the flame again," Ember vowed. "I promise."

Bernie touched Ember's cheek and smiled wearily. "Good daughter," he murmured.

Chapter 7

The next morning, Wade headed to work at City Hall. Music from his headphones vibrated throughout his watery head. He approached the door to his department. He was so into his music that he didn't see the flames burning on the floor – until his bag caught fire.

Wade glanced down. "Ah! Fire. Fire!" He desperately patted at his burning bag. "Ah! Fire!" He stomped on the flames that rose from the floor.

Suddenly, Ember stood up, her body forming from the flames. "Hey. Hey!" she cried until Wade stopped stomping on her.

"Oh, sorry!" he said, stepping back. "You're so hot!" He checked his smouldering bag.

Ember raised an eyebrow. "Excuse me?"

"No!" he said quickly. "I mean, like you're smokin'! No, I didn't mean it like tha—"

"Are you done yet?" asked Ember.

Wade dripped with embarrassment. "Yes, please."

"I'm waiting to talk to your boss," she explained. "So make like a stream and... flow somewhere else." She settled back on the floor, ready to wait.

"Actually," said Wade, "Gale won't be in today. She's a *huge* airball fan, and the Windbreakers are finally in the playoffs! *Toot, toot!*" He pumped his fist.

Ember flared with frustration. "Ugh!"

Wade leant away from her heat. "Okay... well, I just came by because I left my passes for the game here last night."

Ember perked up. "Passes?" she asked, standing tall. "Like, plural?"

Things were looking up...

A short while later, Ember and Wade hurried up the Wetro station stairs into the busy Air District. Ember stared in awe at the throng of Airball fans floating into Cyclone Stadium. The stadium was tall and cylindrical, like a cyclone. The marquee read WINDBREAKERS VS CROP DUSTERS.

The game had already begun inside the stadium as Wade and Ember made their way towards Gale.

High above the stands, fluffy Air players dressed in jerseys passed a ball towards a hoop.

Ember couldn't help watching the exciting game. Then she remembered why they had come – to find Gale. "Where is she?" she asked, scanning the stadium.

"Up there," Wade said, gesturing. "In that skybox."

The Air woman in the skybox swelled like a purple storm cloud. "Come on!" she bellowed at the players and refs.

Fear flickered in Ember's chest, but only for a moment. "Okay," she said, taking a deep breath. "Time to cancel some tickets."

As she made her way towards the skybox, she passed a drink vendor. "Toot-toot juice!" they called. "Getcha toot-toot juice!"

When Ember reached the row of seats behind Gale's box, she stopped. A few Water Elements sat between her and Gale. They would likely boil if she passed by them. Cyclone Stadium was yet another part of Element City that had *not* been built with Fire Elements in mind.

"You'll be great!" encouraged Wade. "This way." He started down the row.

Ember sucked in her flames and followed.

"Excuse me. Sorry. Pardon. Oh, sorry," she said. "Fire girl coming through."

"Jimmy, what's up?" Wade called to a fan. "Wendy!" he greeted another. "How good is it to be here?" Wade seemed to know everyone.

But Ember wasn't making any friends. The Water Elements boiled as she passed.

Finally, she and Wade took their seats behind Gale. "Break some wind!" Gale thundered at the players.

"Hi, Gale!" called Wade. "How you doing?"

Gale glanced back at him. "Look at the score," she rumbled. "What do you think?" Then she blasted the players again. "Blow the *ball*, not the game!"

Ember found the courage to speak. "Yeah, so uh, Gale, my name is Ember Lumen. My family runs a Fire shop... Wade wrote us a bunch of tickets yesterday, and—"

Buzz!

Gale grew even stormier. "What kind of call was that?" she cried at the referee. Then she turned impatiently towards Ember. "Lumen? Yeah, Fire shop with thirty citations..."

Ember shot Wade a look. "Thirty!"

He shrugged and gave a nervous laugh.

Ember turned back to Gale. "Anyway, friend, I was hoping we could work something out—"

As the buzzer sounded again, she thundered at the ref. "Come on, ref! Are your eyes in the back of your head?"

On the field above, the Air ref's eyes rotated to the back of his puffy head and he glared at Gale. As the crowd booed, Gale's cloud darkened.

"Oh, no," warned Wade, as if he knew what was coming.

Ember did *not* see what was coming. She tried again. "Yeah, bummer," she said to Gale. "Okay, so the thirty citations—"

"Do you mind?" Gale thundered. "There's a *game* going on." She whirled back around and muttered under her breath, *"Fireball."*

Ember couldn't believe her ears. Her flames flickered. "Fireball?" she repeated. She stood and stepped in front of Gale, blocking her view.

"Actually," said Ember, "I do mind. This is my *life* we're talking about, not just some game."

Gale swelled like a thundercloud. "Some game?" she repeated, her lightning flashing. "This is the *playoffs*. So forgive me if I don't want to hear a sob story about the problems of some little shop."

Ember's flames shot higher, streaked ominously with purple. "Well, that 'little shop' matters *way* more than a bunch of overpaid cloud puffs blowing some ball around."

Gale loomed over Ember, leaning forwards until they were nose to nose. "I dare you," Gale bellowed. "Say 'cloud puffs' one... more... time."

Ember didn't back down. "Cloud," she said. *"Puffs."* She stood so close to Gale that her hot words blew away Gale's nose.

Furious, Gale reformed her nose. As the crowd booed, Wade checked the game. "Oh, no!" he murmured.

Gale looked, too, and gasped.

"Huh?" said Ember.

"Lutz!" cried Wade.

He gestured towards one of the Windbreakers, who raced to guard the net just as a Crop Duster player blew forwards with the ball. *Whoosh!* The ball blew right through Lutz's cloud, straight into the net.

As the crowd booed, Lutz's spirit sank.

"Lutz man," said Wade. "He's been in such a funk 'cause his mum has been sick."

As if to prove Wade's point, an opponent stole

the ball from Lutz. Boos rose from the agitated Windbreaker fans.

"That is so not cool," said Wade, surveying the crowd. "He's doing his best."

Wade suddenly stood and shouted skywards. "We love you, Lutz!" He gestured for other fans to join the chant. "We love you, Lutz! We love you, Lutz! C'mon! We love you, Lutz! Everybody!"

The crowd responded. Soon the chant rose from the stands. "We love you, Lutz! We love you, Lutz!"

Lutz glanced at the cheering section and smiled.

By now, the whole stadium had picked up the cheer. Then Wade started doing the wave. *"Whoooaaa..."* he cried as he rippled his watery body up and down.

Every Water Element in the stands followed suit. A tidal wave of Water Elements rolled around the stadium. When it made its way back to Ember, she opened her umbrella to shield herself from the splash.

On the court, Lutz was energised. He slammed the ball into the net. Score!

The crowd leapt to their feet. Even Ember got caught up in the moment. "Ah, yes!" she cheered. "Yes!"

"Woo!" cried Wade, tearing up with emotion. "Way to go, Lutz!"

Lutz raised his fluffy arms in victory.

As Wade continued to cheer for Lutz, Ember stared at Wade for a moment. *He* was pretty amazing, too. He had inspired the whole crowd to support Lutz, which had turned the tide of the game.

When fans started high-fiving, Wade laughed and joined in. "Uh! Yeah!" he said, slapping his watery palm against theirs. "Woo-hoo!"

But when he tried to high-five Ember, she raised an eyebrow. Fire and water were a danger to each other. What awful things might happen if they touched?

"Oh," Wade said, lowering his arm.

He reached over and gave himself an awkward high five with his other hand. *Smack!*

Chapter 8

After the game, rowdy fans poured out of the stadium. Drums pounded out a victory song while fans cheered and laughed.

"Woo-hoo!" cried Gale. "What a comeback!"

"Check out who found the gift shop!" called Wade. He was covered head to toe in Windbreakers gear. He waved a foam hand and shouted, "Woo!"

Ember grinned. "I gotta admit," she said to Gale, "that *was* pretty cool."

"You can see why I can get all churned up," said Gale. "But as a 'cloud puff' who used to come here with her dad, these wins mean a little bit more."

"And as a 'fireball' who's supposed to take over her dad's shop…," began Ember. She hesitated. The words weren't easy to say out loud. "I sure don't want to let him down. And I could use a win, too."

Wade saw Ember's soft, colourful light shine through. She was finally letting her guard down.

"Now I just gotta stop the water from coming in—" she continued.

"*Water?* In *Firetown?*" said Gale.

"Yeah?" said Ember, confused.

"Water was shut off to there *years* ago," said Gale. "Forget the tickets. I'm gonna have to take apart your dad's shop to figure out what's going on!"

"You can't!" cried Ember. "My dad put his *whole life* into that place!"

"*Argh,*" Gale grumbled to Wade. "I bet this is connected to that fluffin' leak."

Wade explained to Ember, "We've been trying to track down a leak in the city. It's why I was in the canal and – wait!" He whirled around to face Gale. "I know where I got sucked into Ember's shop! Ember and I could track the water from her shop and find the source of the leak!"

Gale looked intrigued. "Keep talking," she said.

"I could call in a city crew to fix whatever we find," Wade said.

Ember jumped on board. "Yes!" she cried. "And there'd be no need to touch my dad's shop!"

Gale churned that over, then smiled at their hopeful faces. "You're lucky you're a cute couple," she said.

Ember's cheeks burned. "Oh, we're not a—" she said quickly.

Gale cut her off. "You got until Friday. If you can find the leak and get a crew to fix it by then, those tickets are forgiven. If not? Your dad's shop gets shut down." With those last words, Gale drifted off to join the flow of cheering fans.

"Thank you!" Ember called. She looked at Wade, who was still wearing *way* too much fan gear. "Please take all that off," she said.

"But I got you a hat!" he cried, plunking a Windbreakers hat onto Ember's head.

Poof! It instantly burnt up.

"Okay," said Wade.

That night, Ember and Wade stood outside Bernie's shop, where Bernie wouldn't see them. Ember knew her father wasn't a fan of Water Elements. But she needed to work with Wade to track down the source of the leak.

"Just keep outta sight, okay?" asked Ember. "It'd be a whole thing."

Just then, Bernie's voice bellowed from above. "Now there's water upstairs?" he cried.

Ember and Wade peeked through the shop

window. Bernie had ripped a piece of plaster from the wall, revealing another leaky pipe. "It's in the walls," he groaned. "I don't understand! I fix one pipe and another one leaks!"

Bernie rushed to move the Blue Flame out of harm's way. "Ah, water!" he grumbled as the leaky pipe sprayed water across the room.

Bernie threw open the window. As smoke billowed out from his wet flames, he began coughing. Ember and Wade pressed themselves to the wall so he wouldn't see them.

When Bernie left the window, Ember whispered to Wade, "How could it be worse?"

"Now that water's back, the pressure is forcing it up to *all* your pipes," Wade explained.

"We gotta find the source!" replied Ember. She and Wade crouched down to look through the basement window, and then at a pipe that led from the shop to the culvert and into the floor of the canal near her house.

"How did you even end up here?" Ember asked.

Wade recalled the moment clearly. "Well, I was in the canals, checking the doors for leaks... when I found some water that shouldn't have been there." He had dipped his finger in the puddle and tasted it. It was rusty, with a hint of motor oil.

Suddenly, a rush of water had knocked Wade off his feet. Then he got sucked into a filtering system. Then, *bam!* He'd got jammed into a pipe that was clogged with debris.

"But then I heard this explosion…" Wade described the vibration that had shaken the pipe, breaking up the debris. He had burst out and come face to face with Ember. "That's how I ended up at your place."

Ember sighed. She knew the exact source of the 'explosion' Wade had heard. "Oh, flame, my temper caused this?" Ember gazed at all the canals in the distance. "So we're searching for water 'somewhere' in a canal?" she groaned. "Those canals go *everywhere*."

Wade agreed. "It's why tracking down that leak has been so dang hard."

Ember simmered over this, trying to think of a plan. Then she glanced upwards.

"The roof!" Ember said suddenly. It would give them a *much* better view.

Chapter 9

From the rooftop of Bernie's shop, Ember and Wade looked out over the canals. But to get an even better view, Ember knew they needed to be higher.

She slid a tarp off part of the chimney, which was topped with a smoke cap. When she melted the smoke cap off its stand, it toppled, nearly hitting Wade. He yelped and darted out of the way.

Ember tied the tarp to the upside-down smoke cap. "You might want to step back," she warned. Then she threw the tarp high over her head and blew flames into it. The tarp inflated. Ember had made a makeshift hot-air balloon!

Wade gazed up in astonishment. "Holy dewdrop!" he exclaimed.

"Shh!" said Ember, hoping her father wouldn't hear. "Get in."

Wade climbed into the smoke-cap basket of the

'balloon'. As it rose into the air, he stared at Ember with wonder. Her beautiful blaze shone bright, and he was so close to her now, he could feel her heat. When his arm started to boil, he reluctantly leant away.

As they floated above Firetown, Wade recognised the spot where he'd got sucked into the pipes. He pointed towards a puddle, one of many that led up that canal. "More water. Go that way!"

Ember steered the balloon. As they passed the darkened window of a tall building, her light illuminated two Earth Elements inside who were picking each other's fruit. They froze.

"Nothing weird going on here," called one.

"Uh, just a little pruning," said the other.

Wade and Ember shared a laugh, and then fell into an awkward silence as they floated away from the window.

"So, uh, what do you do at the shop, if you don't mind me asking?" inquired Wade.

"My dad's retiring," Ember explained, "and I'll be taking over. Someday, when I'm ready."

"It must be nice knowing what you're gonna do," said Wade. "After my dad passed, I got all 'What's the point?' Now I just go from one job to the next."

Ember gazed into the darkness. "There's a word in Firish," she said. "*Tìshók*'. It means embrace the light while it burns, 'cause it won't always last forever."

"Tee-shook…," Wade said carefully, trying to accurately repeat the word.

Ember hid a smile. "Or something like that," she said.

As the balloon rounded a large building, the main part of Element City came into view. Ember spotted a familiar building and her shoulders slumped.

"You okay?" Wade asked.

"Yeah," she fibbed.

"You sure?" asked Wade.

Ember glanced downwards. "It's just… that building over there?" She pointed. "That's Garden Central Station."

Ember began to recall a childhood memory. "When I was a kid, my dad took me there because they had a Vivisteria tree. I'd always wanted to see one. It's the only flower that can thrive in *any* environment. Fire included."

Ember remembered the sign advertising the blooming Vivisteria. She had grabbed her father's hand and run towards the station. But as they'd approached the entrance, a guard had stopped them.

"I was so excited," Ember murmured. "But they said our fire was too dangerous and they wouldn't let us in."

Ember remembered how furious Bernie had been. *"Tsh'à ts' shâ sh pfùkh, tkhò ts'? Khû kò shá sh!"* he had hollered. "How dare you keep us out? Shame on you!"

"Go back to Fire Land!" the guard had shot back.

Everyone in line had laughed. "My dad was so angry and embarrassed," Ember said. "The building flooded a few years later, so I missed my one chance to see a Vivisteria."

When she turned towards Wade, she was surprised to see tears in his eyes.

"You must have been *so* scared," he said.

"I was," Ember said softly. Then she shook off the uncomfortable memory. "How do you do that?" she asked.

"Do what?" Wade asked.

"Draw people in!" said Ember. "You got a whole stadium to connect with you. I can't even connect with *one* customer. My stupid temper always kicks in." She drooped over the side of the basket.

"I guess I just say what I feel," said Wade. "And I don't think a temper is so bad. Sometimes when I

65

lose *my* temper, I think it's just *me* trying to tell me something I'm not ready to hear."

Ember lifted her head. "That's ridiculous."

"Maybe…," admitted Wade. Then he pointed at something below. "Hey, there! Put us down there!"

Ember steered the balloon towards a culvert. They landed and climbed out beside two giant wooden doors that were slightly ajar.

"That's not right," said Wade, studying the doors. He dipped his finger in the water nearby and tasted it. Then he started to gag. "Motor oil," he confirmed. "Yup, this is the source!"

He led Ember through the doors to investigate and headed towards the main canal.

"Why's there no water?" asked Ember.

"Because the doors are broken," Wade explained. "This is supposed to catch spillover from those main canals, and—"

Just then, a giant cruise ship rolled by. Its wake triggered a small tsunami over the canal walls.

Wade panicked. "Run for your life!" he cried.

They raced towards the culvert doors. Ember jumped through to safety, but Wade was caught on the other side, clinging desperately to the door. "Ahhh!" he cried. "Help! Ahhh!"

Ember blazed into action. She melted a piece of rebar off the door and thrust it towards Wade. "Grab this!" she cried.

He grasped it and she tugged him through the door to safety. Then Ember saw the steaming tops of Firetown buildings in the distance – exactly where the rushing water was heading. "Firetown!" she said with a gasp.

She raced out of the culvert towards a pile of sandbags and picked one up. "Catch!" she called.

Wade turned just as the sandbag hit him. *Bam!* It splattered him to the ground, but he rolled back up to his feet. He struggled against the flow of water to carry the sandbag towards the broken doors.

Water still poured through the doors. With gritted teeth, Wade carried the sandbag with one arm and used his free arm to press against the flow of water. His body undulated against the pressure, but he was able to push the water back.

Finally, Wade heaved the sandbag towards the base of the doors. Then he called up. "Ember! Throw me more!"

They piled on sandbags, one by one. Ember threw them down and Wade stacked them up. When the bags were piled high, the water *finally* stopped. They set the last sandbag in place – together.

As Ember caught her breath, she studied the bags. "So, will this hold?"

Wade pushed against the bags, testing them. "Yup, it should for sure. At least long enough for me to get a city crew to fix it before Friday."

Ember didn't catch every word. She was too distracted by a clump of sand stuck to Wade's face.

He caught her staring. "What?"

"You've got a little... sand," Ember said, pointing.

"Oh." Wade poked around in his face, trying to find it. "Here? Here?"

Ember reached out, nearly touching his cheek. "It's right there," she said. "Um..." She yanked her hand back before she made him boil.

"Oh." Wade plucked out the clump of sand. "Thanks."

They fell silent for a moment, their eyes locked.

"Well... let me know when it's done, I guess," said Ember.

"I'll make sure there's a city crew here by Friday," said Wade.

"Okay," she added. "See ya." She turned and started to walk away.

"Wait!" Wade blurted. He lowered his eyes, suddenly nervous, and asked, "Any chance you're free tomorrow? To hang out with a Water guy?"

"With a Water guy?" Ember smiled. "My dad would boil you alive."

"He doesn't have to know!" Wade insisted. "We could meet in the city. I promise nothing weird… Maybe a little pruning?" he joked, shrugging his shoulders.

Ember laughed, but then she caught herself and stopped. "Sorry," she said, turning away. "That's not going to happen."

"You smiled!" Wade called after her. "I saw it! Tomorrow? I'll be at Alkali Theatre. Three o'clock!" He grinned.

Ember kept walking. Wade couldn't see it, but she was smiling, too.

Chapter 10

At Bernie's shop the next afternoon, Flarry and Flarrietta sat at their regular table playing chess. Buckets hung overhead to catch dripping water. A trickle of water dripped onto the chessboard, snuffing out a fiery piece.

"Oh!" cried Flarry. "Your ceiling is dripping again."

"More leaks?" Bernie grumbled, glancing up.

"Don't worry," said Ember. She hopped onto a table and melted the leaky pipe shut with her hands. "This whole problem is going away. I can feel it."

Ember hopped down. Then she checked the time. It was almost three o'clock – time to meet Wade!

"And since we're all good, I'm also going away... to do deliveries!"

As Ember rushed past her mother, Cinder sniffed the air. Her face lit up. "Do I smell something on... *Ember*?" she exclaimed, laughing with glee.

Her daughter was finally in *love*. Cinder was certain of it.

As Ember hurried out the front door, Clod suddenly appeared. "Yo, Ember!"

"Ah, Clod!" she said, startled.

"I grew another one!" he announced. He popped a tiny flower out of his armpit, then offered it to Ember. "My queen."

Ember touched the flower and again... *poof!* It burned up. "Oops, sorry," she said. "But gotta go." She left Clod behind and hurried towards the cinema across town.

Wade was waiting for her beneath a marquee that read TIDE AND PREJUDICE. When he saw Ember coming, he teared up. She had actually come! He tried to pull himself together as they headed into the theatre.

When the lights dimmed inside, Ember's flames shone bright. *Too* bright. All around her, audience members scowled. She pulled her hood tightly around her flames and slunk into her seat.

After the film, Wade and Ember wandered along the street, stopping at a photo booth. Wade made goofy faces, but Ember's glow blew out the exposure. The only thing visible in the photos were two sets of white eyeballs.

Later, they boarded a lift to an observation deck that looked out over the city. As more people crowded into the lift, Ember and Wade squeezed together so close, they were nearly touching.

When they arrived on the deck, a few kids shrank from Ember's flames. But she knew how to put them at ease. She blew smoke rings that transformed into silly faces.

As the kids cheered, Ember took a bow. Wade gazed at her with watery, adoring eyes. The kids seemed to like Ember almost as much as he did.

Almost.

The next day at Bernie's shop, Ember sat at the counter with a notebook. Inside, she doodled ideas for a new sign. She also snuck glances at the photo strip of her and Wade tucked beneath the notebook.

When a customer lit a sparkler before buying it, Ember grabbed it from him. Her flames churned, but she took a breath to compose herself. She calmly handed the sparkler back to the customer.

As Ember stole another glance at Wade's photo, Bernie walked up, startling her. Had he seen the picture? Ember covered it up with her notebook and a nervous smile. When Bernie walked away, she sighed with relief.

But Cinder had seen everything. When Ember left the counter, Cinder snuck over and lifted the notebook. She studied the photo strip.

"Who *is* this guy?" Cinder wondered aloud.

She was determined to find out.

Ember and Wade hung out again, this time at an outdoor café. A waiter breezed past, dropping off mugs of a pink drink. Wade downed his in one gulp – and immediately turned purple.

Ember tried to drink hers, but the liquid boiled away before it even touched her lips.

Suddenly, people around them started dancing. It was a flash mob! Wade hopped up and bounced his sloshy stomach to the music. He waved for Ember to join him.

Wade stretched like a stream around Ember's flickering moves. Then people started coupling off and dancing together. When Wade held out his hand to Ember, she froze. She wanted to take it, but how could she? Her heat would boil him! She was relieved when a couple danced by too closely, knocking Wade backwards into a fountain.

He emerged seconds later, spouting water from his mouth and posing like a fountain statue. Ember couldn't help grinning a little.

The next time Ember and Wade met up, they strolled around Mineral Lake, where colourful crystals grew along the shore. When Ember stepped on a crystal, her orange flame turned green.

"Whoa," said Wade. "How'd you do that?"

She picked up the loose crystal. "It's the minerals," she said. "Check this out." Ember raced along the lake, her fire changing colours based on which mineral she stepped on.

Wade laughed out loud. "Awesome!"

As Ember leaped onto a high cluster of crystals, he blew out his breath. "Wow." Then he had an idea. "Watch this!"

Wade raced onto the surface of the lake and skidded across, spraying a fine mist in the air. The mist caught the sun's rays and reflected a rainbow of colour.

When Wade came to a stop, Ember – all aglow – gazed at him. He was definitely starting to grow on her.

Later, when Ember walked home alone under the elevated Wetro, it whizzed overhead, sending a wall of water down from the track. But this time, Ember didn't pop an umbrella.

She longed to touch the water. She reached out her hand but hesitated a moment too long. The water vanished as the train disappeared along the tracks.

Bernie's shop lay just beyond the tracks. Ember pulled her flames together and hurried through the door into the familiar shop.

But the next day, in the culvert uptown, water began leaking through the sandbags she and Wade had so carefully stacked. And that water began to slowly flow towards Firetown.

Chapter 11

The next morning, a shallow river of water raced through the canal near Bernie's shop. Inside, Bernie struggled to make kol nuts while Ember climbed to a high shelf to get something for a customer.

"*Sòbê sh sfá*," said the customer. "I'll take that one."

"Another?" asked Ember.

"*Ìshkshá*," replied the customer. "Please."

Ember reached for a bottle on the top shelf just as the walls of the shop rumbled and shook. A chunk of drywall fell off the wall and crashed to the floor near the Blue Flame. Water gushed from a pipe in the wall shooting out towards the Blue Flame.

Bernie hopped to his feet, desperate to save the Flame.

"No!" cried Ember.

"The water is back!" Bernie hollered.

Together, they struggled to move the Blue Flame. Bernie began to cough.

As Ember melted the leaky pipe, someone called from the door. "Ember Lumen? Delivery for Ember Lumen?"

A delivery person entered carrying several vases of flowers. From across the room, Ember could see two eyes in the water inside one of the vases.

Cinder reached the delivery person first. "Flowers for Ember?" she said in a giddy voice.

Ember gasped. She finished fixing the pipe and hurried to collect the flowers. "Oh, excuse me. Hee-hee, these are beautiful," she said. "I'm going to put these away." She darted towards the basement.

As Ember set the vases on the basement floor, she whispered, "What are you doing here?"

Wade popped his head out of a vase. "I got bad news," he said as he began pouring water from the other vases onto his head. With each pour, he grew taller and his body filled out. "The sandbags didn't hold."

"Uh, obviously!" said Ember.

"Yeah. And I also got worse news." He pulled some flowers from his head and tossed them to the floor. "I'd forgotten a *tiny* detail about the last time I saw that city crew."

Wade explained how his ex-boss had reminded him of something. "You knocked over three tons of cement dust," his ex-boss had said. "Half the guys still haven't recovered!"

Wade could still picture the angry construction workers – Water guys who had frozen like statues as the cement dust coating their bodies eventually hardened.

"I guess you could say they still have *hard* feelings," he said, chuckling at his own joke. "Because they won't help us."

"Wade," said Ember, "Gale's deadline is tomorrow. We need more sandbags!"

"But that didn't work before," Wade reminded her.

"Well, I can't just do *nothing*!" Ember fired back, exasperated.

Suddenly, the basement door burst open. "Ember, did you fix the leak?" her father called as he started down the stairs. Bernie gasped when he saw Wade. "It's you again!"

Wade glanced over his shoulder, as if Bernie were talking to someone else. "Who, me?" Wade asked, confused.

"You're the guy who started all this!" shouted Bernie. He grabbed a fireplace poker and swung it at Wade.

"Ahhh!" yelled Wade.

"No, Dad!" said Ember. "Different guy. Not all Water looks alike."

But Bernie looked at Wade's badge. "You are a city inspector?"

Wade glanced down, busted. "Uhh…"

"No!" Ember answered for Wade. "Right?" She shot Wade a look, willing him to play along.

"Right," Wade confirmed uncertainly. "I am not an inspector." He put his hand over his badge, but his water only magnified it. The word *inspector* grew larger.

Wade tried again, covering the badge with his other arm. But the word grew even larger.

Bernie stared at it. "You *are* an inspector," he said. "Why are you poking around? Is this because of the water leak?"

"No!" said Ember. "Not because of water in *any* way. He's a different kind of inspector. Right?" She glanced again at Wade.

"Yeah, yeah, I'm a…" He fumbled to find the words. "I'm a… *food* inspector. I've come to inspect your food." He stood tall, trying to look official.

"Hmm," Bernie said to Ember. "I think he's lying through his feet."

"Teeth," corrected Ember.

"Whatever!" Bernie said. Then he turned back towards Wade. "The food is upstairs. Come."

As Bernie led the way upstairs to the shop, Ember shot Wade a look. "Food inspector?" she hissed.

"I panicked!" he whispered.

Ember grunted with frustration.

In the shop, Bernie slammed a bowl of burning kol nuts on the counter in front of Wade. Wade gulped and laughed nervously.

"Are you really a food inspector?" interrogated Bernie.

"As far as you know, yeah," Wade said.

"Then inspect *this*," said Bernie, gesturing towards the burning kol nuts.

Ember stepped forwards. "Dad...," she began.

Bernie silenced her. He pushed the bowl closer to Wade.

Wade leant over and sniffed. His nostrils bubbled from the heat. "Yep, looks all good to me," he confirmed.

"No," said Bernie. "Inspect it with your mouth." He demonstrated by eating a kol nut and blowing fire.

Wade smiled weakly. He scooped up a kol nut with a spoon. He blew on the nut as if that would make any difference. Then, as the customers in the shop held their breath, he took a scalding bite.

Everyone watched as the kol nut sizzled down Wade's clear, watery throat. Then the pain hit him, and his smile disappeared. Wade let out a scream before clamping his hands over his mouth.

Bernie watched with a satisfied smirk as a massive air bubble rose through Wade's face.

Pop! It burst a hole in the top of his head, releasing hissing steam.

"You see?" Ember said quickly. "He likes it!"

Wade started coughing, but then he stopped himself, holding it in. He smiled and gave a thumbs-up. When he tried to speak, he could only nod. His throat was burning.

Bernie laughed and reached for another bucket of kol nuts. These were even hotter than the others. "You must try these. They're straight from Fire Land." He poured some of the kol nuts into Wade's dish.

"Dad, those are too hot," Ember cautioned.

"I'm okay," croaked Wade. "I love hot food."

He took another bite, and his head filled with air bubbles. *Pop! Pop! Pop!* Water burst from the holes, forcing Wade backwards. He sprayed water all over the shop.

"Hey, watch your water!" cried Bernie. "So, did we pass?"

"Mm-hmm," said Wade. "*A*-plus." He straightened up. "Actually, after the heat dies down, that's really good." He pointed at the kol nuts. "If you don't mind…"

Wade grabbed a cup and scooped up another portion of kol nuts. He dripped water onto them from his finger, and the nuts smouldered and hissed.

Ember gasped. She cleared her throat, trying to get Wade's attention. This was going to burn her father up! She slid her hand across her neck as if to say, *Cut! Stop! Please!*

But Wade didn't take the hint. He took a drink from the mug and smacked his lips. "See, it's really tasty if you water it down a little…"

"Water us down!" Bernie exploded. "Water us down! Where's the camera?" He pulled an instant camera from behind the counter and snapped a photo of Wade's terrified face.

"We will *never* be watered down by you," declared Bernie. "Get out!"

Ember hurried towards Wade. "All right, sir," she said. "You gotta go."

As Wade backed out of the shop, Bernie was still huffing and glaring.

"Dad, don't worry," Ember called to him. "I got this." She followed Wade out the door.

Bernie let loose a string of Firish as they left.

"Look, meet me at the beach and we'll make more sandbags," said Ember outside the shop. "We have to figure out how to fix those doors."

They locked eyes for a moment, and then Wade hurried away.

Back inside the shop, Bernie was still seething. "Water wants to water us down?" he said. "Then water is no longer allowed in the shop!"

He pinned Wade's photo to the wall under a Banned sign. "He is panned!" Bernie declared.

"Um... banned," Ember gently corrected.

"Banned!" echoed Bernie. He was so agitated, he started coughing intensely.

Ember had never seen her father cough so hard. She rushed to comfort him. "*Àshfá*, it's okay," she soothed. "It's all going to be okay."

But as she glanced up at Wade's photo on the wall, she wasn't so sure.

Chapter 12

That night on the beach, as the sun was setting, Ember shovelled sand into a bag. It was exhausting work, but she was determined.

Wade held the bag open. "I don't think this is going to work," he confessed.

"Well, it won't unless you hold the bag straight," Ember argued.

Wade adjusted the bag. "Maybe your dad will understand," he said gently.

Ember scoffed and continued shovelling.

"I'm serious," said Wade. "Look, I know it can be tough. I mean with my dad... we were like oil and water. I never got a chance to fix that." His voice was heavy with regret. "But you guys are different. It might be time to tell him."

Ember shovelled faster. "Yeah, right," she said. "And tell him what? That I got us shut down and destroyed his dream?"

Ember let out a furious yell. Then she collapsed to her knees. Her fire simmered to a soft, gentle candlelight. As she calmed down, her prismatic inner light showed through.

"I think I'm failing," she murmured. "My *àshfá* should have retired *years* ago, but he doesn't think I'm ready. You have no idea how hard they've worked or what they've had to endure. The family they left behind…" She paused and then finally asked the question that was burning in her heart. "How do you repay a sacrifice that big? It all feels like a burden. How can I say that?"

Ember sank lower and hung her head. "I'm a bad daughter," she whispered.

Wade crouched beside her. "Hey, no," he said. "You're doing your best."

Ember sniffed. "I'm a mess," she said with a small laugh. She fired up her flames, trying to cover her vulnerable light.

"Nah," said Wade. "I think you're even more beautiful."

When he grinned, Ember smiled back. "Maybe you're right when you said my temper is trying to tell me something," she admitted.

That was when Wade noticed the sand beneath Ember. "Whoa, look what your fire did to the sand," he said. "It's glass!"

Ember picked up a piece of glass and melted it in her hands. She formed it into a sphere and created a design inside, something that reflected how she was feeling.

Wade watched her, mesmerised. He had never seen anyone do something like that before. "It looks like a Vivisteria flower," he said.

Suddenly, Ember had an idea. "I know how to seal those doors!" she announced. She hopped up and started to run, leaving the glass Vivisteria in the sand.

Wade followed close behind, wondering what this amazing Fire girl had in mind and how he could help her.

When darkness fell, Ember and Wade were working at the culvert. Ember stood before the stack of sandbags holding the doors shut. She inhaled deeply and pressed her hands against the bags, and then there was an explosion of light.

But this time she controlled her blast, as if she were painting with fire. Ember glowed with joy.

Wade admired her radiant light as she worked. She seemed so... free.

When Ember finished, she stood back and

caught her breath. She had melted the sand into a thick wall of glass! She sighed with satisfaction. But Wade bit his lip. He sniffled, and then he let the tears flow.

"Are you crying?" Ember gently teased.

"Yes!" he sobbed. "I've just never been punched in the face with beauty before."

Suddenly, the earth began to vibrate. Ember gasped as an enormous boat passed through the canal, sending sheets of water into the culvert.

Ember and Wade stared at the glass wall as the water rushed in behind it. They took a couple of steps backwards, ready to run. But the glass held. Water splashed only into the bottom of the culvert behind the doors.

"It worked!" cried Ember.

"I'll have Gale come by right after work," Wade promised. "I'll let you know the second I hear anything."

"You think this'll be good enough for her?" Ember asked.

"Honestly?" said Wade. "It's hard to know. She could go either way."

Ember nodded nervously. Then Wade took something out of his pocket very carefully. "Oh, here… I saved this for you," he said, handing her the glass Vivisteria. "It's special."

Ember silently accepted her creation. Had she really made something so beautiful?

The next night, Ember sat in her room, admiring the glass Vivisteria. She turned it over and over in her hands. Then she heard her father coughing.

Ember hurried downstairs and found Bernie repairing a wall. When he coughed again, she asked, "*Àshfá*, you okay?"

Bernie smiled. "Yes, yes. There's just too much to fix."

Ember pulled a metal stool towards him and took a seat. "I'll take care of it," she said. "*You* need to rest. And that's an order." She gave him her most stern expression.

"Yes, ma'am!" Bernie saluted.

They both laughed, and then Bernie took her hands. "Ember, I see a change in you," he said. "Happier. Calmer with customers, and with that… *food inspector.*" He spat the last two words as he glanced at Wade's photo on the wall.

"You're always putting the shop first," Bernie continued. "You have proved I can trust you." Then he began to cough again. His hand flickered, but he quickly hid it from Ember. "I'm so lucky I have you," he said before starting up the stairs.

Ember's smile faded. She stared at the picture of Wade on the 'banned' board. Had he heard back from Gale yet? She had to find out. She had to see Wade right now.

Chapter 13

Cinder, who had been sleeping, suddenly sat upright and sniffed the air.

Cinder sniffed again. "Love!" she declared.

Downstairs, Ember locked the shop door and snuck towards her scooter. She quietly pushed it away from the shop, then started the engine and drove off.

Cinder followed her out the front door. She suspiciously sniffed the air and headed after Ember, following her scent.

Ember drove to Water Town, where canals flowed freely and ice-blue buildings streamed skywards. When she reached Wade's mum's flat, she glanced up at the grand entrance, which was surrounded by cascading waterfalls. Ember gulped.

A large Water guy with a moustache guarded the front door. Ember hurried towards the door just as Wade opened it. "Ember!" he said. "You found it! Everything okay?"

"Please tell me that you have some good news from Gale," she said. "I'm getting really worried about my dad. This has to break my way."

"Yeah, I haven't heard from her yet," said Wade, "but she *swore* she'd call tonight. Actually, my family stopped by for dinner. You want to come up and wait for the call together?"

Ember hesitated. "Your family?" she said.

Just around the corner, out of view, a member of Ember's own family was hot on Ember's trail. Cinder sniffed the air and caught Ember's scent. When she saw Ember talking in the doorway of the large building, Cinder ducked. Who was Ember talking to? Cinder peered over a ledge but couldn't quite see.

"Okay, I'll come up for a bit," Cinder heard Ember say.

As Ember gazed up again at the ritzy building, she caught her breath. "I'm sorry, you *live* here?" she asked Wade.

He shrugged. "It's my mum's place."

"Oh my gosh," said Ember. She followed him into the building, past the Water doorman.

Cinder hurried up to the doorman and tried to walk in, too. "I'm afraid I can't let you in," he said. "Residents and guests only."

She pretended to leave, then spun sideways and

tried to dodge the doorman. But he extended his arm, creating a wall of water.

Cinder spun the other way and he blocked her again.

"Ah, okay. I *understand*," she said. "You're surprisingly good at your job!"

"You're surprisingly fast for your age," he responded.

"You have *no* idea," Cinder warned. As she spun her flames into a small tornado, the doorman's eyes widened.

Upstairs, Wade's mum, Brook, warmly greeted Ember. "Ember! I'm so excited to finally meet you," said Brook. The tall, elegant Water woman leant forwards. "Do we hug, or... wave, or... don't want to put you out. Ha, ha!"

"Um," Ember smiled nervously, "a hello is fine."

"Hardly," Brook argued. "Wade hasn't stopped talking about you since the day you met. The boy is smitten!"

"Mum!" cried Wade, mortified.

"Oh, come on," said Brook. "I'm your mother. I know when something's lighting you up. I just didn't know she would be so *smoky*!" Brook faked a cough at Ember's 'smokiness', and they all laughed.

Ember stopped laughing first.

Ember's mother, **Cinder**, is a matchmaker who can smell love in a Fire Element's smoke. If only her daughter could find a match...

When Wade is pulled into the shop's basement through a gushing pipe, he is forced to write several tickets. The shop could be shut down! **Ember has to stop Wade!**

Ember Lumen is a quick-witted Fire Element with a hot temper. She helps her parents run the family shop, the Fireplace.

Wade Ripple is an empathetic Water Element who bubbles with compassion. He works at City Hall as an inspector.

Ember pleads with Wade to cancel the tickets. He offers to help her. They visit **Fern Grouchwood's office** in the processing department.

Ember and Wade try to convince Fern to **cancel the tickets**, but...

... Ember's **fiery temper** ignites Fern's office! What's worse, he is still able to process the Fireplace's tickets.

Ember is given a brochure called *So Your Business Is Being Shut Down*. Wade feels terrible.

Next, Ember and Wade decide to ask Wade's boss, **Gale**, to cancel the tickets. They find her at an airball game.

Gale offers them a deal: if they can find the source of a water leak in the city and fix it, **she will tear up the tickets**.

Wade goes in for a celebratory high five but forgets one very important thing:
Fire and Water can't touch!

Wade and Ember search for the source of the leak. They spend time together and
discover that **they enjoy each other's company**!

At **Mineral Lake**, Ember has a special moment with Wade. When she steps on a crystal, her flame matches its colour!

Wade shows Ember that he can make **a rainbow**. He also shares his perspective on life, which prompts Ember to question her own path.

Ember walks back to the Fireplace after spending the day with Wade. **She really likes him**, and she has never felt this way before.

Cinder performs a smoke reading that will reveal Ember's and Wade's feelings for each other. Is it true love? And if it is... **can Fire and Water be together**?

"Come this way," said Brook, waving them inside. "Meet the rest of the family."

Ember followed, until she saw that the flat was one big swimming pool filled with floating furniture. It was not designed for Fire Elements. In fact, it felt a little dangerous.

Wade reached for a golden floaty chair and held it so that Ember could climb in. But it was too flammable. So Wade covered it with the less-flammable welcome mat from the foyer.

Ember finally made it into the chair, but she wobbled precariously.

As Wade guided Ember into the pool, Brook exclaimed, "Oh, honey! You won't believe what your baby niece did today! She... she smiled." Brook immediately teared up, which got Wade going, too.

"No, she didn't," he blubbered.

Brook nodded, and then they both burst into tears.

Ember stared, wide-eyed. Wade's family was so different from her own.

When they followed Brook through a waterfall curtain, Wade held his arm above Ember to keep her dry. They emerged into a dining room full of Water Elements sitting at an inflatable dining table.

"Hey, everyone!" said Wade. "This is Ember!"

"Hey!" said a Water guy who looked a lot like Wade. He wore a chef's apron and a cheery smile.

"That's my brother Alan," said Wade, "and his wife, Eddy."

Eddy, a curly-haired woman in a jumper, waved at Ember. "Hi!"

"And we got two kids that are swimming around here somewhere," said Alan. "Marco!"

A young Water boy popped out of the water.

"Polo!" Alan called again.

Another kid emerged. "Hi, Uncle Wade!" Polo hollered.

When the kids saw Ember, they stared. "Do you die if you fall in water?" Marco asked. He jostled her floaty chair.

"Whoa!" said Ember.

"Marco!" Wade scolded.

Alan flushed with embarrassment. "Kids, hee-hee," he said to Ember. "Don't hate us."

As the kids swam away, Ember regained her balance – and tried to smile.

"Anyway," said Wade, pulling her floaty towards the dinner table, "that's my little sib, Lake. And their girlfriend, Ghibli."

"'Sup," said Ghibli, peering at Ember from beneath a swoop of hair.

"They're students at Element City School for the Arts," Wade explained.

"Following in Mum's wake," added Lake.

"Oh, nonsense," said Brook, waving her hand. "I'm just an architect. The real artist is my brother Harold."

Harold, a short, broad Water man, held Polo under his arm. "Oh, I just dabble in watercolours," he said. "Or, as we like to call them, 'colours'."

Brook placed a dish on the table and sat down. "Oh, don't listen to him," she said. "He's a wonderful painter. One of his paintings just got in the Element City Museum's permanent collection."

"Wow," said Ember. "That is so cool. My only talent is 'Clean-up on aisle four'."

Wade scoffed. "Talk about being modest. Ember's got an incredible creative flame! I've never seen anything like it." He cast her a loving glance.

Harold looked at Ember, too. "I just have to say," he said, a bit too loudly and slowly, "that you speak *so* well and clear—"

Wade shot his uncle a look, but Ember kept her cool. "Yeah, it's amazing what talking in the same language your entire life can do," she said.

"Doh!" said Harold, embarrassed at his inappropriate comment.

Alan quickly changed the subject to break the tension. "Hey, Ember, did Wade ever tell you that he's deathly afraid of sponges?"

"No," said Ember, intrigued.

"I was traumatised," said Wade.

He explained how at nursery school, he had been walking with his class when a janitor dropped a huge sponge. Curious, Wade touched it with his finger – and the sponge began sucking in his water. He had tried to pull away, panicking, but the suction was too strong. It soaked him up entirely!

When Wade finished the story, everyone laughed except him. Even Ember let out a chuckle – she couldn't help it!

"I still can't use a sponge around him!" said Brook.

"I was stuck in there for hours," said Wade defensively.

Alan reached for a pitcher, but he was laughing so hard, the pitcher slipped from his hand and shattered.

"Alan! That was new!" his mother scolded.

"My bad," Alan apologised. "I'm all whirlpools tonight."

Ember picked up two large shards of glass and blew on them, melting them back together. "I can fix it," she reassured Alan. She gathered the rest of the broken pieces and melted them into a glowing liquid orb. Then she blew it into a shape resembling a pitcher.

As Ember worked, her inner light cast rainbows across the room. She was so lost in her creative process, she barely noticed that everyone was watching her.

With one last twist and pull, Ember formed the handle of the pitcher. She tweaked the spout and set the pitcher back on the table. Then she saw the others staring.

Ember zipped up her fire. "Oh, um, sorry," she said quickly.

"That was incredible," gushed Harold.

The whole family began cheering and applauding.

Ember's face burned. "It's just melted glass," she said modestly.

"Just melted glass?" echoed Brook. "Every building in the new city is built from 'just melted glass'."

Ember glanced out the windows for the first time and admired the view of the Water District. Brook had a point.

"Oh, no," added Brook, "you have to do something with that talent."

Wade leant towards Ember. "See?" he whispered. "I told you you're special."

Ember smiled back, suddenly believing him.

Then Wade got an idea. "Ooh, thought bubble!"

he announced. "Maybe after dinner we play the Crying Game?"

Excited murmurs circled the table.

"Let me guess," said Ember. "You try to cry?"

"We try *not* to cry," Wade corrected her.

After dinner, it was game time. Brook and Harold faced off against each other first. Wade flipped over a timer and said, "You have one minute. Go!"

Harold spoke first. "Nineteen seventy-nine. November. You—"

Brook instantly burst into tears. Her team – Wade, Lake, and Eddy – threw up their hands while the other team – Alan and Ghibli – celebrated.

"—never got a chance to say goodbye to Nana," bawled Brook before Harold could say another word.

"Okay, Ember, Wade," said Harold. "You're up."

Ember and Wade faced off.

"Yeah, this is almost unfair," Ember pointed out, "because I have literally never cried. You've got no chance."

"Sounds like a challenge," said Wade with a grin.

Harold flipped the timer. "Ready, go!" he declared.

"Butterfly. Windscreen wipers. Half a butterfly," Wade said simply.

His family sniffled and sobbed, but Ember sat still as a statue, unmoved. So Wade tried again. "Okay, an old man on his deathbed remembers the summer he fell in love. She was out of his league, and he was young and scared." Wade sniffled, his own words getting to him. "He let her go, thinking surely summer would come again." He sniffled again. "It never did."

Wade did his best to hold back his own tears. But still, Ember's eyes were dry.

"Almost out of time," Harold blubbered.

Wade realised he was going to need a different approach. He tried again. "Ember, when I met you, I thought I was drowning. But that light, that light inside you, has made me feel so alive. And all I want now is to be near it – near you. Together."

He stared into Ember's eyes, which reflected his own image back at him. He looked deeper, so deep that he could almost see her there beside him, shedding her outer light.

As he gazed at her, he saw something startling. A white-hot lava tear drop rolled down her cheek and landed in the water with a *hiss*.

For a few seconds, no one moved. Wade, Ember, and Wade's entire family were caught up in the moment. Then...

Ring! Ring!

The phone broke the silence.

Wade hurried to pick it up. "Hello?" he said. "Gale, hi."

Chapter 14

Across town, Gale stood at the culvert with a few Air city workers. "Glass?" she said into the phone to Wade. "You repaired it with glass?"

Gale watched as an Air worker tested the glass by punching it. *Poof!* His hand disappeared. Another worker raised a hammer, about to hit the glass.

"Hold the storm…," said Gale, watching.

On the other end of the line, Wade swallowed hard. Ember anxiously waited.

Gale saw that the glass held against the force of the hammer. "*Tempered* glass?" she said. "Solid as a rock. I like it. Consider the tickets cancelled."

As Wade hung up, he broke into a teary-eyed smile.

"We did it?" Ember incredulously asked.

"Yup!" said Wade.

Later, when it was time to go, Ember approached

Wade's mother. "Thank you, Mrs Ripple," she said. "This was… this was really great."

Brook held the repaired glass pitcher in her hands. "Yeah, it was," she agreed. "And I mean what I said about your talent. I have a friend who runs the best glass-making firm in the world. During dinner, I slipped out and I made a call. And I told her about you. They're looking for an intern. It could be an amazing opportunity."

Ember glowed with excitement. "For real?"

"It's a long way from the city, but it would be an incredible start," gushed Brook. "You have a bright future." Then she glanced down at the pitcher in her hands. "Look at me! I have an original Ember!"

Ember smiled nervously as she turned to go. An internship at a glass-making firm *would* be an amazing opportunity. But how could Ember ever leave her father and the shop? He needed her.

"Hold up," called Wade. "I'll walk you out."

Downstairs, Cinder was still sparring with the doorman. By now, the doorman was a half-steamed waterwall. Cinder's fiery tornado had slowed to a stop, and she was trying to catch her breath.

"I'm afraid you're still going to have to wait out here, ma'am," the doorman huffed and puffed.

"And I'm afraid…," said Cinder, gasping, "I will throw up." Dizzy from spinning, she staggered towards the bushes right as Wade and Ember left the building.

As Ember hurried towards her scooter, Wade raced after her. "Ember!" he called. "Ember, hold up. What's going on?"

"I can't believe she basically offered me a job," groaned Ember.

"I know!" said Wade. "Could be cool!"

"Yeah, super cool, Wade," she said sarcastically. "I could move out and make glass in a faraway city. Do whatever I want." Her flames roiled.

"I don't understand," said Wade.

"I'm going home," said Ember. She started up her scooter.

"Fine," said Wade, "then I'm going with you." He hopped on back, careful to leave a little space between himself and Ember's flames.

"Ugh!" cried Ember. She revved the scooter, zipping into the night while Wade hung on for dear life.

Cinder regained her balance just in time to see them drive off. "A Water guy!" she exclaimed.

"Look, my mum was just trying to be helpful!" Wade yelled over the scooter's engine. "She doesn't know how excited you are to run the shop!"

"Arrgh!" Ember growled. She revved the scooter again, weaving through traffic so fast that Wade's body began to stretch out.

"What is the matter?" Wade cried.

"Nothing!" she insisted.

"Yeah? Because we're going like a thousand and—" Wade's eyes widened and he gestured wildly. "Bus!"

His body stretched out even more as Ember swerved to avoid the bus.

By the time they reached Firetown, Ember was going so fast that the wind rippled her flames. "You don't know me, Wade! Okay?" she declared. "So stop pretending like you do."

"What is this about?" he hollered.

"Nothing," she said. "Everything. I don't know. It's..."

As they approached Bernie's shop, she hit the brakes and skidded to a stop. Wade's body sloshed back into shape. Through the dark windows of the shop, the Blue Flame flickered.

"I don't think I actually *do* want to run the shop, okay?" Ember admitted. *"That's* what my temper has been trying to tell me... I'm trapped."

As she climbed off the scooter, she stared at the Blue Flame. "You know what's crazy? Even when

I was a *kid,* I would pray to the Blue Flame to be good enough to fill my father's shoes someday. Because this place is his dream. But I never once asked... what *I* wanted to do." She sighed. "I think that's because deep down, I knew it didn't matter. Because the only way to repay a sacrifice so big is by sacrificing your life, too."

Wade searched for what to say to make Ember feel better. But someone else spoke first.

"Ember!" Cinder descended the stairs of the nearby Wetro platform. "Don't move!"

"Oh," muttered Ember. "My mother." She froze as Cinder hurried towards them, stopping a couple of times to catch her breath.

"Mum, it's okay," Ember started. "He's just a friend."

"Si—" Cinder took another breath, holding up her finger. "Silence!" she ordered, so loud that Ember gasped.

"I could smell you from over there!" said Cinder. "You stink."

Ember's face flamed. "What are you talking about?"

"*You* know what I'm talking about," replied her mother.

Ember sniffed herself, and then it dawned on

her. "You're smelling love on me?" She glanced at Wade and wondered… *was* she in love?

"If your father finds out…," Cinder warned. "Fire and water cannot be together! I'll prove it! Come with me."

She led them into her matchmaking office, where Ember and Wade sat across from Cinder. On the table between them lay two sticks.

"I will splash this on your heart to bring love to the surface," Cinder explained. She splashed Ember with oil, a little forcefully.

Then Cinder splashed Wade, leaving an oil slick on his watery surface. Wade flinched, but then felt a pleasant sensation.

Cinder gestured towards the sticks. "And then you must light these with your fire and I will read the smoke."

Ember lit one stick with her flaming finger. But Wade gulped and looked at his finger. He had no way to light the flame.

"See, Ember?" said Cinder. "It cannot be."

"Actually…," said Wade thoughtfully. He moved until he stood between Ember and the sticks.

"What are you doing?" Ember whispered.

Wade pulled up his shirt. His clear, watery surface refracted Ember's light, as if he were a magnifying glass. When he focused the beam of light onto the stick, the stick burst into flames.

Both Cinder and Ember blinked with surprise.

The intermingling smoke from the sticks turned into a double helix. Cinder sniffed the smoke as it rose. Ember watched it, too. Could the smoke actually tell them something?

"Cinder?" Bernie called from upstairs. "Cinder? Who's down there?"

Ember was horrified. "It's my dad. You have to go!" She and Cinder rushed Wade out the door just as Bernie came downstairs.

"Wait, are we a match?" Wade asked as the door closed. When his hand got caught, he yelped and pulled it out. Then he reluctantly headed home.

"What's going on?" asked Bernie. "I woke up and nobody was upstairs!"

"It was just me," said Ember. "I was... double-checking the locks. And Mum came down, and..."

"Yes, and we...," Cinder said, her eyes darting around the room, "began looking at this door. We don't talk about this door enough!"

"Pull it together!" Ember hissed at her mother.

Bernie smiled. "Well, since you are awake... I was going to tell you tomorrow, but I'm too excited to sleep. In two days, I retire!"

"Oh!" said Ember.

Cinder gasped. "Oh, Bernie!"

"Two days?" asked Ember with a gulp.

"Yes," said Bernie. "We are going to throw a *big* party. A grand reopening! That way I can tell the whole world my daughter is taking over."

Cinder clapped, overjoyed, but Ember could only smile weakly.

Bernie took Cinder by the hand and spun her around.

"And I have a gift for you," Bernie announced to Ember. "I've had this for a while, but after our talk, I know now is the time." He pulled out a large box from behind the counter. Then his face grew serious. "Before I give it to you, I need you to understand what it means to me."

Bernie recalled the day when he and Cinder had boarded a boat that would take them to Element City. "When I left Fire Land," he began, "I gave my father the *'Bà Ksô',* the Big Bow. It is the highest form of respect. But my father did not return the Bow, he did not give me his blessing. He said if we left Fire Land, we would lose who we are."

"They never got to see all of this," Bernie sadly continued, gesturing around his shop. "They didn't get to see that I *never* forgot we are Fire. This is a burden I still carry."

Cinder's eyes welled up with tears.

"Ember," said Bernie, "it is important that you know you have *my* blessing every day you come in here. So I had this made for you."

He opened the package and revealed a sign that read EMBER'S FIREPLACE.

Ember was stunned. "Wow, *Àshfá*," she said, her eyes wide.

Bernie flared up, full of youthful energy. "It's gonna be big, bright! Everyone is gonna see this. Ember's Fireplace! We will unveil it at the grand reopening!" He chuckled happily.

Cinder, fearing Bernie might exhaust himself, took him by the hand. "Come, Bernie, you need your rest," she said. She shot Ember a look as they passed.

Ember sat on the floor, alone in the shop, staring at the sign. Her flame dimmed as she began to quietly cry.

Across town, a wave of water spilled into the culvert. The glass dam Ember had created still held, but the water had risen nearly to the top. Under the pressure of the immense amount of water, a tiny crack appeared in the tempered glass.

Chapter 15

The next day, Wade heard a knock on the door of his mother's flat. He opened it and was thrilled to see Ember, who was holding a box.

"Ember!" he said. "So, what'd your mum say? About our reading?"

"Nothing," she said. "Look, I have a gift for you." She waved him into the hall, and then she handed him the box.

Wade reached in and gently pulled out the Vivisteria glass. He stared at it, still mesmerised by its beauty. "And you came all the way here to give it to me?" he murmured. Then he noticed the sad expression on her face. "Wait, why are you giving me gifts?"

When Ember looked away, Wade suddenly sensed she was here to end things. "Oh, no," he said sadly. His eyes fell to the Vivisteria glass, and then he remembered something.

"Hold on," Wade said quickly. "I think I have something to show you. Just give me two seconds! I have to call Gale! And you're going to need a pair of boots!"

Soon after, Wade led Ember towards the deserted Garden Central Station. Along the way, they passed a faded sign advertising the Vivisteria flower – the same sign Ember had seen when she was little. Now the sign had a banner across it, announcing that the exhibit was closed.

"Wade, what are we doing here?" asked Ember.

"Just wait!" said Wade. He stopped in front of a chain-link fence. When he took off his shirt, he was able to walk right through the fence.

Ember walked through the fence, too, but when she did it, she melted the metal.

"Why do they even have these?" asked Wade.

"Eh, who knows," said Ember.

They hurried towards the station. A sign that read NO FIRE still stood in the entryway, keeping Fire Elements out. Wade knocked it over as he passed.

The train station had clearly been closed for a very long time. Only a few ornate tiles remained on the walls. Water dripped from the ceiling, and the entrance stairs vanished into a dark, flooded tunnel.

There, in front of the tunnel, stood Gale. She waved. "Hey! It's my favourite fireball!"

Puzzled, Ember waved back. "Hey, Gale." She glanced at Wade. "What's going on?"

"I know you think you have to end this," he began, "but that flooded tunnel? It goes to the main terminal."

"Okay?" said Ember.

"Do you still want to see a Vivisteria?" Wade asked.

He gave Gale a signal. She inhaled deeply and blew a huge bubble in the water, big enough for Ember to climb into. Gale held the bubble closed at the water's surface.

Ember was stunned. "Wait, I'm supposed to get in there?" she asked.

"The air should last…," said Wade.

"… at least twenty minutes," Gale added.

Ember hesitated.

"*They* said you couldn't go in there…," said Wade. "Why does *anyone* get to tell you what you can do in your life?"

Ember's brow furrowed. She looked at the bubble. Then she looked at Wade. She stepped to the edge of the water.

Gale blew even more air into the bubble, and Ember jumped in. Gale sealed it so no water could leak inside. Then Ember steadied herself and looked out at Wade, who gave her two thumbs up. It was working!

Wade gently grabbed the bubble and started swimming down the flooded staircase. From the surface, Gale waved goodbye.

With Ember in her protective bubble, Wade swam through the dark tunnel. Surrounded by water, Ember started to panic a little. But she remembered that Wade was by her side and she felt calmer.

On the other side of the tunnel was the old train station. Inside the station, Ember's light illuminated the walls. This part of the station was gorgeous. Somehow preserved underwater, the tiles were still beautiful, and so was the vaulted ceiling overhead, crisscrossed with green trellises.

When Wade and Ember explored an old subway car, her glow startled a school of fish. As the fish swirled around her bubble, she laughed.

They followed the fish up a staircase, which opened into a grand ballroom. In the middle, growing in a double helix, rested the Vivisteria plant.

The dormant plant was without any flowers.

But as Wade pushed Ember closer and her light illuminated the vine, it bloomed!

"A Vivisteria," whispered Ember. It was even more beautiful than she had imagined. As she floated up the vine, her light cast colourful prisms, and more flowers bloomed.

Ember gazed at the purplish red blossoms – until another school of fish sent her bubble spinning. "Whoa!" she cried, laughing.

As she laughed, her flames grew brighter, and even more flowers bloomed! Ember lit up with joy, and the vine exploded with flowers. She and Wade continued to swim through the beautiful vines, sharing the magical moment.

But suddenly, the bubble around Ember began to shrink.

The flames on the top of her head were now touching the inside of the bubble. "Ouch!" she cried.

"Hey!" Wade gasped. "You're running out of air!" He frantically searched for an exit. "That way," he declared. He pushed Ember's bubble towards a narrow stairwell.

As the bubble tightened, Ember started to pant, taking short little gasps of air.

"Almost there," said Wade. "Try to breathe

slow and steady." He pushed her bubble upwards, swimming with all his strength.

Finally, they saw light. They broke through the old subway entrance just in time, landing on the pavement near Mineral Lake and collapsing.

As they lay side by side, Wade's eyes were wide with regret. "I'm so sorry," he said. "I should never have—"

Ember sprang to her feet. "Are you kidding?" she said. "That was *amazing*. I finally saw a Vivisteria!"

"It was inspiring," Wade agreed. "*You* were inspiring." He held out his hand, his gaze steady.

Ember turned away. "No, Wade, we can't touch," she said.

"Maybe we *can*," he said.

Ember stared at the lake. "No," she said again.

"But can't we just prove it?" Wade pleaded.

She glanced at him. "Prove what?"

"Let's see what happens," he said, throwing his arms wide, "and if it's a disaster, then we'll know this would never work."

"But it actually *could* be a disaster," Ember reminded him, her voice rising. "I could vaporise you. You could extinguish me. And then—"

Wade cut her off. "Let's... let's start small." He held out his hand again.

Ember hesitated. Then she tentatively reached towards it, hovering her hand over his. When Wade's hand began to bubble, Ember yanked hers back.

But they tried again. This time, they were able to touch – pressing their palms together. Water boiled and steam hissed. But they were okay.

Ember gasped. She pulled her hand away and examined it. Wade studied his hand, too. They were amazed.

They stepped closer and pressed their palms together again, more firmly this time. Wade's water pushed back to match the strength of Ember's heat. Their hands tingled as they interlocked fingers. They had reached an equilibrium. *They had changed each other's chemistry!*

In that magical moment, in each other's arms, they began to dance.

Wade leant into Ember and closed his eyes. "I'm so lucky," he whispered.

Those words sparked a memory in Ember. Someone else had said similar words to her – her father. "I'm so lucky I have you," Bernie had said that night in the shop.

She could picture him standing beside the Blue Flame with her, a proud smile on his face. Then she remembered how exhausted he was. He couldn't go on like this for much longer.

The sign Bernie had given Ember flashed on and off in her mind: EMBER'S FIREPLACE.

At that thought, Ember zipped up her fire, covering her beautiful, vulnerable light. She pulled away from Wade. "I have to go," she said.

"Wait, what?" asked Wade with confusion. "Where are you going?" When she hurried up the Wetro stairs, he followed.

"Back to my life at the shop," Ember said. "Where I belong. I take over tomorrow."

Wade jumped in front of her. "Whoa, whoa, hold up. You don't *want* that. You said so yourself!"

"It doesn't matter what I want," Ember replied weakly.

"Of course it does!" cried Wade.

She darted around him, up the Wetro stairs, but Wade followed. "Listen," he called after her. "*Listen! You've* got an opportunity to do something you *want* with your life!"

She whirled around on the station platform. *"Want?"* she repeated. "Yeah, that may work in your rich-kid, follow-your-heart family. But getting to 'do what you want' is a luxury. And not for people like me."

"Why not?" asked Wade. "Just tell your father how you feel. This is too important. Maybe he'll agree."

Ember rolled her eyes. "Oh, ha. Yeah." There was absolutely no way she would do that.

Wade set his jaw. "Funny," he said. "And this whole time I thought you were so strong, but it turns out... you're just afraid."

His words ignited Ember's fire. "Don't you *dare* judge me," she said. "You don't know what it's like to have parents who gave up *everything* for you."

Wade looked at her sadly.

"I'm *Fire,* Wade," Ember continued. "I can't be anything more than that. It's what I am, and what my *family* is. It's our way of *life.* I cannot throw all of that away just for *you.*"

All Wade could say was "I don't understand."

Ember glowered. "And that alone is a reason this could never work. It's over, Wade." A train pulled into the station and she quickly boarded it, leaving Wade alone on the platform.

But inside the train, she stopped short. She took a shaky breath, trying to hold back her tears. Then she armoured up, pulling her hood tightly over her flames.

Chapter 16

The night of the shop's grand reopening party, a stage stood outside the shop, lit by hanging lights. The whole community gathered for the big event. Customers sat at outdoor tables, snacking on hot kol nuts.

Bernie wanted everything to be perfect. He had even closed the shop for a few days to prepare.

Ember, in a ceremonial gown, sat on the stage with Cinder. Bernie carried the Blue Flame lantern and placed it on a pedestal nearby.

"Everyone, welcome!" Bernie said. "It is good to see your faces. I am honoured to have served you. But it is time to move on." He gestured towards Ember. "Come."

Ember stood next to her father.

"My daughter, you are the Ember of our family fire," Bernie said affectionately. "That is why I am so proud to have you take over my life's work."

He touched a rope, which burnt like a fuse towards a tarp covering the new sign on the front of the shop. For a moment, it looked as if the entire shop was ablaze. But when the smoke cleared, Ember's sign glowed in all its glory.

As the audience cheered, Bernie looked at Ember. "Pretty good trick, huh?" he said. Then he held out the Blue Flame lantern. "This is the lantern I brought from our old country. Today I pass it on to you."

As Ember reached for the lantern, she hesitated, feeling the weight of the moment. But just as she was about to take it, she heard a familiar voice.

"I thought of other reasons," someone called.

Ember looked up to see a train passing. Then she noticed Wade standing in front of her and gasped.

"Wade?" she said, shocked.

The members of the crowd murmured to one another.

Cinder swallowed hard. "Oh, boy," she said under her breath.

"What are you doing here?" Ember asked.

"You said me not understanding is the reason we can never work," explained Wade, choosing his words carefully. "But I thought of other reasons. A bunch of them. Like, number one: you're Fire, I'm Water. I mean, come on. That's crazy, right?"

A Fire Element in the audience nodded in agreement.

"Who is this?" Bernie asked.

"No idea," Cinder fibbed unconvincingly.

"Number two," Wade said, "I'm crashing your party. Like, what kind of a jerk am I?"

"A pretty big one," admitted Ember.

"Right?" said Wade. "Number three: I can't eat your... delicious foods!" To demonstrate, he took a mug from one of the outdoor tables. He swallowed its contents and strained to speak, his head bubbling with the heat. "*Very* unpleasant," he croaked.

Bernie suddenly recognised Wade. "Wait, I know him!" he said to Cinder. "He is the food inspector!"

"Oh, right!" Wade continued. "Number four: I'm banned from your father's shop. There are a *million* reasons why this can't work. A million no's. But there's also one 'yes'. "

He stepped closer to Ember. "We touched," he said. "And when we did, something happened to us. Something *impossible*. We changed each other's chemistry."

As he gazed into Ember's eyes, she smiled.

But Bernie jumped towards them, exasperated. "Enough!" he cried, his voice yanking Ember back to reality. "What kind of food inspection is this?"

Wade stood his ground. "A food inspection of the heart, sir," he replied.

"Who are you?" asked Bernie, jabbing his fiery finger at Wade.

"Just a guy who burst into your daughter's life in a flooded old basement," Wade said.

"So you *are* the one who burst the pipes!" accused Bernie.

"What?" said Wade, taken aback. "Not me, it was..." His eyes involuntarily darted towards Ember.

Ember's eyes widened. It was too late. The damage had been done.

Bernie looked sadly at Ember. "You?" he asked, his eyes narrowing. "*You* burst the pipe?"

"I—I—" stammered Ember.

"Ember—" Wade started to say.

"Silence!" Bernie bellowed.

"No!" cried Wade. He pleaded with Ember. "Take the chance. Let your father know who you really are."

Ember was speechless.

"Look," said Wade. "I had regrets when my dad died, but because of you, I've learnt to embrace the light while it burns." Then he recited in perfect Firish: "*Tìshók*'. You don't have forever to say what you need to say. I love you, Ember Lumen."

Party guests gasped, but Wade continued. "And I'm pretty sure you love me, too," he said softly.

Ember looked into Wade's eyes. She was completely torn, but she had to make a decision. She put up her fire wall, trying to hide behind it.

"No, Wade," she said flatly. "I don't."

At that moment, in the culvert, the crack in Ember's glass dam grew larger.

Wade's heart felt as if it were cracking, too.

"That's not true!" Cinder argued with Ember. Then she faced Bernie. "I did their reading!" Cinder confessed, throwing her arms in the air. "Bernie, it's love. It's true love."

"No, Mum," said Ember, "you're wrong. Wade, go!"

"But, Ember—" he protested.

Ember flared as hotly as she ever had. "I don't love you!" she hollered.

At this, another crack sliced through the glass wall. Water started to spray out. Any moment now, the dam would blow.

"Go!" Ember cried again, purple with anger.

Wade, heartbroken, removed the glass Vivisteria from his pocket. He placed it on the stage at Ember's feet. Then he walked away, his shoulders sagging.

Bernie glared at Ember. "You have been seeing *Water*?"

"*Àshfá,* I—" she tried.

Hurt and betrayal flickered across Bernie's face. "You caused the leak in the shop?" he said. "I *trusted* you!"

Ember's flames burned with shame.

Bernie began to cough. "You will not take over the shop. I no longer retire." He grabbed the lantern and stormed into the shop, with Cinder following close behind.

Ember stood alone onstage as party guests began to quietly leave, their subdued flames disappearing into the dusk. She stared sadly at the glass Vivisteria.

When the guests were gone, Ember was consumed with sadness. She climbed onto her scooter. She drove through Firetown and onto the bridge. She parked, removed her ceremonial gown and stared at the bright lights of Element City in the distance.

Ember remembered the moment when she and Wade had touched for the first time – how they had danced at Mineral Lake. She pulled the glass Vivisteria from her pocket and sighed. Then she looked back at Firetown. "Why can't I just be a good daughter?" she asked herself aloud.

Her frustration flared, and she wound back her arm to throw the Vivisteria into the water. But she couldn't bring herself to do it.

Ember stared again at her mirror image in the

glass Vivisteria. She could see parts of Element City and Firetown in the glass, too. Suddenly, a flash of light reflected in the Vivisteria. It was coming from the culvert in the distance.

"Firetown!" Ember cried.

The glass wall she had built at the dam had shattered – she was certain of it.

Pent-up water began gushing down the culvert, straight towards Firetown. A deluge was headed for her father's shop.

Ember raced to her scooter and took off.

Chapter 17

Inside Grand Gateway station, Wade purchased a ticket. "Well, one-way ticket to anywhere but here," he said sadly.

His family had gathered to say goodbye. "Go! Travel the world. Heal that broken heart," blubbered Brook. Then she began to sing. "My little drip-drip baby boy. Drip, drip, drip goes the baby boy..."

Wade's eyes welled up.

Harold started crying, too. "I made you a painting," he said. "It's of a lonely man awash in sadness."

The painting depicted Wade, standing at the station, just as he was right now. Wade burst into tears.

Through a doorway, he spotted steam rising from Firetown. One by one, the lights of the town flickered out. "Ember," Wade murmured. Was she in trouble?

Ember was already racing her scooter back across the bridge towards Firetown. Down below, she could see her parents in front of the shop, cleaning up from the party. "Mum! Dad!" she cried. But they couldn't hear her.

A wall of water rushed down the culvert. The river slammed into the elevated Wetro track, which came crashing down.

Ember pulled off from the bridge and raced the raging river towards the shop. But now water was filling the street!

She revved the scooter and bravely soared across the culvert. "Water's coming!" she hollered to any Fire Elements in her path. "Watch out! Behind you!"

All around her, Fire Elements began to panic and run to safety.

"Climb! Climb!" Ember cried, urging them towards higher ground. "Flash flood! Hurry!"

As she neared the shop, she shouted to her parents. "Mum! Water! Get to higher ground!"

Cinder, who was helping Bernie clean up the stage area from the grand reopening, instantly grabbed Bernie. She tugged on him to go.

Then Ember's scooter hydroplaned, with waves splashing upwards. It sent a streak of pain up her leg. The water in the street was getting too deep to ride her scooter. She leapt off it and onto the cab of a pickup truck. Would she be able to reach the shop from here?

Water lifted the stage, carrying Bernie and Cinder with it. Bernie lunged towards the shop. "The Flame!" he cried.

Cinder held him back.

"Let me go!" yelled Bernie.

Then he saw Ember jump onto floating debris that carried her towards the shop. She was risking her life to save the Flame.

"Ember, no!" he cried.

She took one more leap through an open window above the shop's front door. Water was already gushing in.

Crack!

Ember gasped as the front door began to give way. Spouts of water jetted in around the door, flowing towards the Blue Flame.

Ember threw her weight against the door. The rising water nipped painfully at her feet.

Suddenly, through the glass of the door, two eyes appeared. Ember heard a muffled grunt. "Wade?" she said.

His face materialised, smushed against the glass. He gestured towards the door handle. "Keyhole!" he cried in a muffled voice.

Ember yanked the key from the lock, and Wade squeezed in through the keyhole. "Gahhh!" he cried.

Inside the shop, he reformed his body. "I was hoping to make a more heroic entrance," he said.

Then he sprang into action, joining Ember at the door. Side by side, they held back the wall of water.

"You came back after everything I said," said Ember.

"Are you kidding? And miss all this?" he joked.

Ember smiled – until she saw that the rising water in the shop had nearly reached the Blue Flame. "Hold the door!" she cried.

Ember jumped along counters and shelves until she reached the Flame. She piled sandbags around the base of the cauldron. Then she flared up and made glass from the melted sand.

Outside the shop, Bernie and Cinder clung to the stage as violent water churned all around them. Debris rushed down the street, smashing cars and knocking down street lamps. The sign tumbled off the front of Bernie's shop, narrowly missing them.

Back inside, as water rose, Ember quickly built a glass cylinder around the Blue Flame. "No, no," she pleaded, hoping the glass would hold.

Wade struggled to hold the door in place as windows and pipes began to burst. Water rose faster, covering the family photos on the wall. The lantern that had carried the Blue Flame from Fire Land was swept up in the flow.

"Ember, we have to go!" cried Wade. "We have to go *now*!"

"I can't leave!" cried Ember.

"I'm sorry to say this," said Wade, "but the shop is done. The Flame is done."

"No!" cried Ember. "This is my father's whole life. I'm not going anywhere—"

Smash! Water roared through a brick wall. A shelf toppled and slammed into the glass cylinder, breaking the glass and exposing the Flame.

The base was cracked, the Flame weak. But it wasn't out. Ember climbed up on a box to avoid the rising water. "Throw me that lantern!" she shouted.

Wade spun in a circle, searching, and then swam for the lantern. Then a huge wave swept him sideways. "Ah!"

The wave pushed Ember and the base of the Blue Flame towards the old fireplace hearth. Debris piled up, sealing Ember inside. She gripped the base of the Flame, but when she glanced down, she saw that the Flame was extinguished.

"No!" cried Ember.

Just then, the debris shifted. Wade popped into the hearth, and he was holding something. It was the lantern – with the Blue Flame inside! Wade handed it to Ember.

"Thank you," breathed Ember. "Thank you." Then she flinched in pain. "Ahhh!"

Water had seeped into the hearth and splashed onto Ember's knees. She studied the blocked entrance and saw water trickling in through the cracks.

Ember used her heat to melt the debris and seal the cracks. Her efforts stopped the leaks, but also created a lot of heat. It was now so warm in the hearth, Wade began to boil.

"It's too hot in here," he said.

Ember looked up at the chimney stack, which opened to the sky above. "Climb!" she ordered. She went first, and Wade followed.

But before they could reach the top, a car cascaded down the water-filled street and crashed into the shop, shaking the building. The top of the chimney collapsed, sealing Wade and Ember inside.

The space was so small, so tight and so very hot. "Back up! Back up! *Back up!*" cried Ember.

They dropped back down into the hearth, which was even tighter now that more debris had fallen. Wade was steaming.

Ember went over to the blocked entrance. She

heated up again, trying to burn through. It didn't work. And now the room was even hotter.

Wade was evaporating at an alarming rate.

"I have to open that up!" cried Ember.

"No!" said Wade. "The water will come in, and you'll be snuffed out."

"But you're evaporating!" cried Ember. She saw that Wade was full-on boiling now. "I don't know what to do!"

"It's okay," he said calmly.

"No, it's not okay!" she cried.

He took her hand. "Ember, I have no regrets," he said. "You gave me something people search for their whole lives."

Ember cried, pleading with him. "But I can't exist in a world without you! I'm sorry I didn't say it before. I love you, Wade."

Steam surrounded them.

In her sorrow, Ember's most vulnerable light cast rainbows on the wall.

Wade instantly felt a sense of peace. "I really do love it when your light does that," he whispered.

As they embraced, steam continued to fill the hearth.

Silence fell.

Wade was gone.

Chapter 18

When the water receded, Bernie, Cinder and their neighbours pushed through the damp debris, desperate to find Ember.

"They're in the hearth!" cried a Fire Element.

They cleared debris away from the fireplace, knocked through an opening and found Ember.

She knelt on broken bricks and glass, illuminated by the flicker of the Blue Flame. Her own light was dim. "Wade is gone," she said sadly.

Cinder climbed in and held Ember tight. "Oh, my daughter," she soothed.

"He saved me," said Ember. She pulled out of Cinder's embrace and faced her father.

"Dad... this is my fault," Ember said, her voice shaky. "The shop, Wade... I need to tell you the truth."

She took a deep breath. It was time to admit what she had come to realise. "I don't want to run the shop. I know that was your dream, but it's not mine. I'm sorry. I'm a bad daughter."

She handed the lantern with the Blue Flame to her father.

Bernie set down the lantern. "Ember, the shop was never the dream," he said, his voice thick. "*You* were the dream. You were always the dream."

At those words, Ember embraced her father. "I loved him, Dad," she admitted, sobbing now.

Cinder wrapped her arms around them, too. Then Ember heard a familiar whimper.

Condensation had formed in the chimney.

A drop of water, like a single tear, fell into a bucket. Ember glanced up. Could it be?

Then Ember got an idea. She remembered the Crying Game she had played with Wade and his family. "Butterfly...," she said softly. She stared hopefully at the chimney. "Butterfly. Windscreen wipers. Half a butterfly."

She could hear Wade crying softly now. A few more drops plunked into the bucket.

Ember felt a surge of hope. "An old man on his deathbed remembers the summer he fell in love...," she said brightly.

More drops fell.

Ember covered her mouth, crying tears of joy this

time. "She was out of his league, and he was young and scared," she continued. "He let her go thinking surely summer would come again. It never did."

Water fell harder now. Wade was bawling.

Realisation dawned in Cinder's eyes as she gazed upwards. "You are a perfect match," she announced. "Ten out of ten!"

Wade sobbed. As water poured into the bucket, Bernie looked at Cinder. "I don't understand," he said. "What's going on?"

Cinder waved her hand. "Just say something to make the Water guy cry, okay?"

Bernie scratched his head. "Um, uh... you are no longer panned," he said.

"Banned," Wade whimpered.

"Banned," Bernie agreed.

As Wade wailed, a puddle formed on the ground. Ember stepped over to the middle of it. "I want to explore the world with you, Wade Ripple!" she shouted. "I want to have you with me, in my life. Forever!"

Droplets poured down, and then they stopped. The bucket was full. Ember peered into the bucket.

Two eyes peered back. And a smile formed.

Wade stood up. "Whoa," he breathed, suddenly realising he wasn't wearing any clothes. "Your, uh, chimney needs cleaning." He quickly located his shirt and pulled it on.

Ember ran towards Wade, laughing. They kissed for the very first time. Ember glowed a breathtaking purple that lit up the room.

"I *knew* it!" declared Cinder, beaming. "My nose *always* knows."

Even Bernie had to chuckle. Ember looked so happy. How could he not be happy for her?

It took many months for Firetown to recover from the flood. Bernie's shop, now fully restored, bustled with customers. The original shop sign hung above the door. Hot logs spun, lava java steamed and kids crunched on crackly sweets.

Clod, wearing a shop apron, stood on a ladder beside a Fire girl. "If you were a vegetable," he said, "you'd be a cute-cumber." He held up his arm and revealed an armpit flower. He yanked it out, yelping in pain, and presented it to the girl. "My queen."

She giggled.

Gale, dressed in a Windbreakers jersey, browsed the merchandise. "Uh! I can't believe I was gonna shut this place down," she said.

As she gazed at the stocked shelves, she accidentally

backed up into an Earth guy who was also wearing a Windbreakers jersey.

"Whoa! Sorry," Gale apologised. Then she realised who it was. "Fern? You're a Windbreakers fan?"

"Toot, toot," he answered, pumping his fist.

"Toot, toooooot," said Gale, instantly smitten.

Flarry and Flarrietta stood behind the counter now. "Oy, you know what I like best about running this shop?" asked Flarrietta.

"Not having to eat Bernie's kol nuts!" declared Flarry, chuckling.

"Sorry, I couldn't hear you through my retirement," toyed Bernie.

Everyone burst out laughing just as Ember entered the shop. When Bernie caught her eye, they shared a smile.

Wade came in behind her. "Hey!"

Everyone greeted him, including Bernie. "Hi, Wade!" they called good-naturedly.

"Hey, Wade!" called Clod. "Yo, yo, yo!"

Wade laughed and turned to Ember. "Ember, it's time," he said.

She smiled sadly, but she knew he was right. It was time to go.

At the docks of the Grand Gateway, Ember and Wade prepared to board a passenger ship. But first they had to say goodbye to their families.

"You know, I'm not really one for tearful goodbyes," said Wade.

Brook burst out crying. "Oh, Wade," she blubbered, "you big liar. Drip, drip, drip goes the baby boy." She hugged him.

As Wade burst into tears, too, Bernie shot Ember a glance. "Uh, are you sure about this one?" he asked.

Ember grinned. "I'm sure." Then her expression changed. "Dad, I'm sorry the internship is so far away. I mean, it's the best glass-design company in the world, but who knows if it'll become a real job. And it might not end up being anything—"

"Shh," said Bernie. "Go. Start a new life. Your mother and I will be here. And now we have more time for hanky-panky."

"Ê... shûtsh!" scolded Cinder, giving him a playful nudge.

Wade and Ember began to walk up the ramp of the ship, but Ember turned back. She smiled at Bernie and set down her luggage. Then she knelt on the dock. She stretched her arms out long before her and gave Bernie the *Bà Ksô*, the Big Bow.

Cinder gasped at the respectful gesture. But Bernie, tears in his eyes, stepped forwards and returned the bow. He and Ember shared a moment, both feeling a tremendous weight lift. Then Cinder helped Bernie up, and the boat sounded its horn.

It was time for Ember and Wade to go.

Ember hurried up the ramp and boarded the boat behind Wade. Leaving Firetown was difficult, but she had taken the first step long ago – when she had summoned up the courage to follow a Water man onto a train.

Leaving her parents and the security of their family shop was even more difficult. What was ahead for her, across these waters? What did the future hold? Ember didn't know. But with Wade by her side, she was ready to find out.